ALSO BY THOMAS FASANO

The Dead (editor)
A Concise Guide to MLA Style and Documentation
Great Short Stories by Great American Writers (editor)
Common Core Grammar: High School Edition
The Complete Diaries of Adam and Eve (editor)
Adult Coloring Book: Stress Relieving Cityscape Designs

Thomas Fasano

The Arean Wall

COYOTE CANYON PRESS  CALIFORNIA

By th' helm of Mars, I saw them in the war,
Like to a pair of lions, smeared with prey.
—William Shakespeare
The Two Noble Kinsmen

www.coyotecanyonpress.com

Library of Congress Control Number: 2023902131
ISBN: 979-8-9877655-0-0

The Arean Wall

THE ANARCHO PROBLEM

"The destruction of the Anarchos," Arean McAlister said, "is not a solution. It's not even feasible. The real solution is to find a way to live together."

"What's the point of that?" Stephen said.

"You're still talking about this as if it's a battle, a confrontation, a war. The Anarchos aren't trying to defeat us. They're trying to make peace. They're not interested in fighting us. They're not interested in the future of humanity. They're interested in saving their own skins."

"The point is for us to have a future," Stephen said.

"And your plan is what?" McAlister said.

"I say kill them all."

"Even though they're not trying to kill us?" McAlister asked. "They're afraid of us—because they think we're dangerous."

"That's not true," Stephen said.

"You're wrong. I can't think of anything I'd be more eager to prove to you."

"And why?"

"You're not a god," Arean said to his brother. "The people of Mars are not gods. They're a race. They're a species. They're a faction. And they want to keep their faction alive."

"We know all that," Stephen said. "The trouble is, I can't think of any other way to make them go away."

McAlister was still looking at the image of the crowd on the monitor. The door whooshed opened, and Ersa Callisto, Federation scientist and diplomat, stepped out.

"That's her," Stephen said.

"So, you think we should kill them all?" McAlister said loud enough for her to hear.

Stephen didn't answer.

Callisto, a head shorter than McAlister, was austerely dressed in black. Her face was so pale, it seemed almost translucent, but she had a firm jaw and dark eyebrows. "What's the situation?" she said.

"I'm afraid I don't have a clue," Arean said. "The situation is fluid. We need to make the best of it. I don't have a better answer."

"It's not a matter of how long," Stephen said, "but how much. The situation is deteriorating rapidly. The Federation made their position clear when the Anarchos backed away from the treaty. We have no better option than to give up on the treaty and go to war."

"Sorry to hear that, Marshal. This is not the outcome we hoped for. We've been trying to avoid a conflict."

Stephen was never a fan of the military. His time in the service left him with a permanent distrust of the armed forces, and his experiences with the Anarchos had only reinforced that distrust.

From his point of view, the military's presence on Mars was a constant reminder of the Anarchos' power and the threat they posed to humanity.

"It's not just the Anarcho colony we're dealing with here," said Callisto. "We've got to be careful not to antagonize our fellow Discordians."

"They're not the enemy," said Arean. "They're just worried about their own interests."

"I'm not sure I understand," Ersa said.

"Not yet, but you will," Arean said. "It's not what you think. The treaty is a sham. The treaty was signed in the early days of the colony, when it was still a colony. The treaty was intended to prevent it from becoming a war zone. But as the colony expanded, it became obvious the treaty wasn't going to work."

Stephen turned to the man who was standing behind them. "Mr. Brock, we'll need your help with the computer."

"Of course."

Stephen turned back to Ersa. "We'll need you to go with us. You'll be safe."

Ersa felt her throat tighten. She was being taken away from her home, her people, and her children.

"I think we should take a look at the treaty," McAlister said.

"Not now," Callisto said. "That would take too much time."

The treaty was, in fact, a long document. There were several hundred pages, and the text covered a wide range of topics. The treaty began with a long preamble, followed by a long list of definitions, and then a long list of articles, each of which had its own lengthy preamble.

"My guess is you're saying if we don't leave this planet, the Anarchos will kill us all?" Callisto said.

"I'm saying we've got no choice," Stephen said.

"I'm not sure I'm following you," Callisto said. "You're saying the treaty is invalid?"

"The treaty is not a treaty," Stephen said.

"Then what is it?" Callisto asked.

"A piece of paper," Stephen said.

"Yes, but it's a piece of paper many people have signed," Callisto said.

The treaty was a compromise, one that left out a great many things.

"You're not actually suggesting we break the treaty?" Callisto said.

"It's not just the treaty," Stephen said. "It's the whole situation. There're a lot of people who think we should do more to help the people in the cities. So we need to deal with the Anarcho problem now."

Stephen's face was a mask of self-righteousness. He was a man who never had the need to hide his feelings from anyone. McAlister had never seen him so angry.

Callisto's voice was barely audible. "I'm sorry," she said. "We can't break the treaty. Too much progress has been made."

Stephen's eyes were like ice. He tried to keep his voice calm. "We'll consider it," he said. "But I'd like to see that data first."

He gestured at the screen. Mr. Brock was pounding away at the keyboard.

McAlister could see his brother's eyes flicker from the screen to the ceiling and then back again.

"You're a member of the Security Council," Callisto said. "You're supposed to be representing the interests of all humanity."

"All humanity? I'm afraid I can't do that."

"But you're in charge of the mission. Surely, you have the authority to stop it. You're one of the senior members of the Federation."

"The mission is not mine to stop," McAlister said.

"I don't believe that," Callisto said. "Galaxica will be too focused on what happened to her nest to worry about the rest of us."

"So you're saying we're safe?" Arean asked, looking at Stephen, who was making a deep gutteral sound.

Stephen was about to answer, but Arean cut him off. "I'm going to try to persuade Galaxica to give up her plan. I'm sure I can convince her it's not worth the risk."

"And if you can't?"

Silence.

GALAXICA'S GAMBIT

The day before they landed on the planet, the local commander of the Anarchoist forces met with McAlister and Stephen. He was a small, balding man who wore the blue-and-silver uniform of the Anarchoist League. He had a face like a boiled egg and a voice like a foghorn. He made it clear they were not backing down.

McAlister considered the alternative. He did not doubt that the war would continue for a long time; when it did, every man and woman in the fleet would pay the price of victory.

But there was something else he learned in the previous war that he could not share with Stephen.

"You're not going to get us all killed, are you?" Arean asked.

"I'm going to do my best to avoid that," Callisto said. "But there's one thing I don't understand. The war was over. We were at peace. Why are we still fighting?"

"There's always a war going on," Stephen said. "And we're not at peace. Not in the way you mean."

"But we are at peace," Callisto said. "We have the treaty. We signed it. There's no war."

"But there is a war," Arean said.

Callisto turned and looked at Arean's brother. He was a tall man. The light from the shuttle's windows played on the silver stubble of his beard, highlighting the blue of his eyes. He looked every bit the soldier.

"I'm not a defeatist," Arean said. "I'm just realistic. We are not going to get out of this with a treaty, and the only reason we're sending a team down there is that we've got to have some kind of face-saving mechanism. You're just going to have to live with that."

"So what do we do?" Callisto asked.

"We'll do what we've always done," Arean said. "Wait and see."

He sank into the pilot's couch and pulled the helmet down over his head. He had to admit that it felt good to be back in the air and be at a ship's controls again. The war had taken its toll on him, even if he'd been lucky enough to survive.

The ship was already in motion, with inertial dampeners easing the action as it accelerated. McAlister had been in the air for a few minutes before he noticed the vessel was accelerating faster than he'd calculated; the inertial dampeners were not compensating for the increased acceleration. He checked the ship's trajectory and saw it was already decelerating.

"What's happening?" Callisto asked, her voice crackling over the ship's communication system.

"We're being pulled along by a gravity wave," McAlister said.

"Are we in trouble?"

"No," he said.

And for the first time, as they flew over the Martian landscape, he noticed the astonishing detail, the faintest hints of individual habitats, but he could tell that many of them were palaces and mansions. Nowhere was there any evidence of poverty or want. The habitable zone was dotted with what appeared to be meticulously cultivated parks.

It was a place that meant much to him, where he'd watched over for most of his adult life. Nevertheless, that time was ending.

The stars had altered. Before, the firmament was crowded with the remote blue-white spheres of the deep interstellar medium. The void was now an almost seamless field of blackness, scattered with tiny, hard points of light.

McAlister glanced at Callisto. "Galaxica was our only chance. I didn't dare take the risk that she might belying to us."

"I know. But she was. She betrayed us all."

"Yes, she did." McAlister raised his head. "But she wasn't acting alone. She was making a point to the Discordians—us specifically—and the Federation."

"Why did you go to the camp in the first place?" Callisto asked. "Surely you could have avoided it all."

"It wasn't exactly my decision," McAlister said.

McAlister stopped, distracted by the subtle lights of the readout. He tried to interpret the dancing colors. "Is there anything wrong?" he asked.

"You're asking me?" Callisto replied.

Galaxica had told McAlister that her actions would define her as an enemy of war; she would be written into the war's annals. It was a breathtaking gesture. Galaxica was using him to broadcast an act of conscience.

The enormity of what was happening came crashing down on McAlister.

"So you really were set up," McAlister said.

Callisto nodded as if this was some long-awaited vindication. "Galaxica was clever enough to see that letting you go was in her interest. It was a demonstration of goodwill, as far as the war effort was concerned. You must have wondered why I was so keen to see you when you returned."

"So she let you go because you're a better ally than I am?" Callisto said.

"Because she needed to test me," McAlister said. "She's a curious creature. I think she's as close to being insane as I am sane. If there's one thing she hates, it's complacency. She has to experiment."

THE GREAT WALL OF MARS

McAlister was rewarded with only a weak green flash as the shuttle crossed the terminator, and the daylight gave way to a thinning dusk. He flew on. Hours later, McAlister's shuttle crossed a high plateau with deep fractures. The dry ice was thin there, and the exhaust plume threw back colorful lights like the tails of comets. It was a breathtaking sight.

There were signs of habitation as the shuttle approached, things in the air and squirming on the ground. Outside the band of the habitable zone, there was no atmosphere. However, within, the air was so dense that one could walk in it without needing a pressure suit. The wall spanned the desert, a green smile curving across it.

"What about the monoliths?" Callisto asked.

He shrugged. "We're approaching them from the opposite direction, so we should get a closer look soon."

Aurora, their shuttle, orbited the wall at an altitude of a few hundred kilometers. It had been a single-manned spacecraft until thirty years ago.

The body of the wall was a long, thin ellipse that angled down toward the ground along its full length, curving toward its base at the midpoint. It was an extrusion of dust and rocks and sand that covered all of Mars below it, starting in the north and stretching south through *Tharsis Montes* and *Arabia Terra* to *Syrtis Major Planum* in the northwest. McAlister could not see its base from his vantage point, but he knew it lay far below him. The wall had taken centuries to build.

Air whipped through the crystal towers and halls of the wall, a thousand times richer in breathable oxygen than the thin nitrogen atmosphere outside. It was a small, self-contained bubble of life, a miniature of the natural habitat that once covered the planet alfresco.

The air outside was red, thinner, and poisonous, its atoms stripped of the life-giving elements that made up the atmosphere of the habitable zone.

To McAlister, the wall looked as if it had been molded from an enormous porcelain slab, rough and pitted, as if dented by thousands of impacts. The Collapse Civilization constructed the wall over a thousand years ago, before the Transenlightenment. The Collapse was an interstellar civilization that expanded through human-ruled space with a speed unthinkable by modern colonies. They traveled as many as ten light years in a single year using generation ships so vast that each one could include an entire nation within its hull. The Collapse Civilization expanded at such an incredible pace that none of their ships ever returned to Earth's solar system.

The original purpose was defensive: to protect the database of human knowledge. It was built at the edge of an escarpment that fell away into an abyss whose lip was hidden from view by a low cloud deck. The clouds never penetrated the wall; if they tried to rise over the rim, they were ripped apart by some unimaginable force field. It was about four thousand feet high and a hundred and fifty miles at its widest point.

"Why don't we land and explore the base?" Callisto asked. "Maybe there are answers in there we can't find anywhere else."

The boundary was just a line on the map, but it was easy to discern up close: a band of shimmering air. If approached in a vehicle, the air would rip and tear, frying all but the hardiest circuitry. If anyone walked towards it, the air would take hold of them, trying to peel away their suit like a set of rotten clothes. The wall extended beyond sight into the lower atmosphere; the structure was designed to protect Mars from asteroids, a significant hazard.

McAlister stood on the foot of the wall and watched the clouds form and envelope him; it was all that was left of the domed settlements that had once been home to millions of people. McAlister could not help thinking of them as the drowned cities of Atlantis. This would be their only opportunity; after that, there would be no more landings.

McAlister and Callisto were watching from the observatory room of the settlement on the outermost edge of the Great Wall.

"The first colonists coined the name," McAlister said. "They called it the wall because it seemed to wall off the world. It was just like a big dam, holding back water."

Callisto's gaze lingered on the wall, mesmerized by the way it seemed to hold the planet together. "It's incredible," she said, her voice barely above a whisper. "To think that something like this was built so long ago, and still stands today."

McAlister nodded, his eyes never leaving the wall. "It's a testament to human engineering," he said. "And to the power of determination."

In the distant past, when fresh water had become more precious than gold on a planet devoid of rain and filled with liquid methane oceans, the arduous task of transforming Mars into a habitable world had commenced in earnest. The construction of a second and third dam was nearing completion, and a vast belt of highly pressurized water was slowly expanding outward, transforming the desolate wasteland.

Everyone knew that a single accident could derail the entire endeavor, and unfortunately, it occurred sooner than expected. A small section of the wall gave way under the intense pressure as miners and engineers worked tirelessly to create new farmland and a forest belt named Lune. Though the malfunction was fixed in time, an enormous flood surged out of Lune and into the sea, wreaking havoc on lowland towns and villages.

The wall itself was a marvel of engineering, with its inner face heated and its outer face kept in temperature-controlled shade, resembling a massive pavilion sheltering an alien beach. The bright lights that adorned its rough exterior had illuminated Mars for generations, slowly baking the planet into a habitable world.

At the base of the wall, a three-hundred-meter-wide region was kept warm by surplus heat from the shining lights, heat pumps, and pipes pumping water from a buried reservoir into the vegetation's roots. Over the centuries, a tiny residual atmosphere had expanded through heating and thickened enough to support microbes, plants, insects, and microscopic crustaceans that covered the regolith, adapting to the water-poor environment with hardy plants that thrived on the surface, their undersides studded with bright lights.

As the initial atmosphere thinned, they flooded the cells with Oxygen-1, the synthetic variant of the element rich in hydrogen. By the time the wall was completed, the giant balloon had become taut and rigid, and the meadow beneath it smelled of flowers, spices, and happiness, like a carnival come to life.

At the base of the wall, water dripped from a hundred different sources, collecting on a thick layer of rock before it trickled downhill and into the many streams and ponds in the lowland forest. Some of the water collected into small lakes, where a few industrious farmers had built floating greenhouses, complete with water pumps and metal heating panels.

The settlers found themselves trapped on what otherwise was a dying planet, but the hundreds of giant habitats scattered around Mars held back the chaos and dangers of the hostile environment. It would take centuries to complete the terraforming process, and by that time, thousands of people would be living inside the Great Wall, creating an economic engine that would drive the local star systems to exhaustion.

As the wall enclosed all settlements, a thousand generations would have lived and died within it, and it would be the only man-made artifact visible from space. Yet, life struggled to reclaim the scar on the landscape and turn it into something else, with rain softening the days and warming the lands in the habitable zone of the wall, and the air thick with the smells of green plants and dried red dust.

THE ANARCHO NEST

The nest stood proud, a gleaming oval suspended between the sky and the earth. It seemed to ripple with an electric charge, casting an eerie streamer of dust around it. Pale and green, it was encrusted with lichen. Its steel legs were thick and jointed, like the interlocking roots of a strange forest that had long forgotten its divisions and become one.

The Aurora was flying again. The nearest part of the nest was a thousand meters below, and they would have to come to rest on the far side. They were halfway there when they heard a crackling sound behind them. Callisto turned.

"We'll need to fly round to the east of the nest to get anywhere near it," McAlister said.

After centuries of creeping outward from the hidden Mother Nest, the Anarchos had built a nest that was so vast that its lower levels were inaccessible from the surface.

The nest was teeming with life, fed by fusion reactors at the base and water tanks fed by ice-mining. The remainder of the nest was given over to fermentation vats where water was turned into food.

The closest dome to them glowed like a harvest moon. The delicate blue light refracted and warped through the polyhedron. The dome was open to the air, or rather, it had no ceiling. In its interior, McAlister could make out the black shapes of complicated machines, blocky and inhuman.

It was surrounded by a sea of smooth white dust. The wind had scoured the dust into a set of gently curved dunes and stony mountains, which the Anarcho engineers had not bothered to smooth out or pave over with polyasphalt.

A few yards away from him he could see one of the gates. It was an amphitheater of smooth stone steps and three round openings, which reminded him of bull's-eyes.

Looking more closely, McAlister made out a series of portals, tall and narrow arches that flickered with a soft blue light that cast ghostly shadows on the ancient dust.

He couldn't decide which was more intimidating: the vast black sky overhead or the yawning darkness before him.

He knew only twenty Anarcho nests existed, and most of them had been designed by the same person, an engineer named Hester Hubble. She'd designed them for maximum efficiency and minimum energy consumption, but her designs wouldn't really matter when all things were said and done.

The earliest nests had been put together in deep space, using robotic systems that hung in orbit around the red planet. Later, nests were built from the inside out using automated tunneling machines. A massive robotic system called a LEO machine would tunnel down from an orbiting ship to form the hard shell of a new nest.

McAlister nodded. "The other side has changed their tactics, but they haven't changed their targets. All of their attacks are still concentrated on the conscripts and our stations and habitats. We know that. There's nothing clever about it. The Anarchos probably think that if they continue with their basic strategy, we'll lose interest in fighting them."

Callisto nodded. "That's what I thought."

He nodded back. "So we agree on the basics, at least. That's a good start for us."

"Agreed," Callisto said. A great starting point, she thought, although McAlister's eyes were unflinching.

He shook his head. "Galaxica won't come with us."

Her eyes narrowed. "I know that."

"What're your plans?"

McAlister sighed. "I'll talk to Galaxica again."

The aircraft shuddered harder this time, with a distinct twisting motion. McAlister gripped the nearest handrail; Callisto sank into her seat. The shuttle seemed to fall away beneath them, angling down towards a wall of cloud. They were so close now that McAlister could see individual wisps.

The channel clicked off. McAlister let out a slow breath, feeling suddenly heavy. Callisto was already taking manual control of the ship's maneuvering jets, bringing the craft toward the wall. They were in the clouds now, as low as the craft was physically able to fly but still several kilometers above the sea. The heat shimmers rising from the water were visible through the windows. They were now less than a kilometer from the base of the wall.

McAlister heard a muffled roar, like distant thunder. The world lurched; through the prow's windows, he saw the ragged edge of a caldera sliding past, the volcanic depression fringed by a narrow black shelf. The ground ahead shimmered as if seen through heat waves.

"Jesus," Callisto said. "What was that?"

"Thermal inversion," McAlister said. "Something to do with the permafrost melting."

The wall ahead was dark and forbidding, and now that they were closer, they saw that it was riddled with dozens of dark circular apertures. McAlister spotted machinery and vehicles parked around them; clearly, they were entrances to hangars.

Callisto nudged the ship's nose into a steep dive, the exhaust from the maneuver scouring the wall.

McAlister watched the wall slide beneath the carapace of the spaceship. He tried calculating how far the escarpment's edge might be.

"Ninety kilometers, maybe a hundred," Callisto said, answering his unspoken question.

There was a note of irritation in her voice; for a moment, McAlister wondered if he'd pushed things too far. Then he realized it was just her manner, nothing more. He looked at the others. "Are you ready?"

"Yes," said Scorpio, the ship's engineer. "Just tell me when."

"Right." McAlister was relieved that he looked perfectly calm.

McAlister turned to Callisto, seeking a cue. She was staring straight ahead, her face unreadable.

McAlister nudged the control yoke and brought the ship around. The engine exhaust turned from yellow to orange as the main fusion drive came on line, pushing them toward the towering wall of ice and rock.

McAlister watched as another ship, which had been slowly catching up with them, began to overtake them and pass. It looked like a child's toy in comparison to theirs. The Anarcho vessel settled down into the foothills of the escarpment, and two smaller craft came down and were now approaching them.

They came down on the edge of the immense city that filled the cylinder. Skyscrapers had been built down to the bottom of the space station; long tube-shaped buildings reached away from the main cylinder like the spokes of a wheel; conjoined buildings, each as big as a city block, rose from the center of the station at regular intervals—a jigsaw-puzzle pattern of light.

The dropship nosed through the door and into the hangar bay.

"She's sending us to our deaths."

"Perhaps not," McAlister said. "I don't think the plan has changed. It was always intended that we would fly this thing over the nest and attempt to set it down on the far side, out of reach of the war machines."

"So we're going to fly the same plan as Galaxica, just without her knowing it?" Callisto asked.

"Something like that"

The shuttle lurched upwards. McAlister grappled with the controls. "Callisto—" he began.

Suddenly, they saw the slugs.

"Just get us clear," Callisto said. "That's all."

The slug writhed its body as it tried to keep them in range.

It launched itself out of the ground, its rear end thrashing furiously. McAlister applied the shuttle's reverse thrust, and the ship's engines screamed in protest. The slug hit the hull just above the airlock, sending McAlister and Callisto flying into the ceiling. McAlister lost his grip on the stick for a moment, and the impact knocked him unconscious for a moment.

The slug detected the shuttle's exhaust with its buried sensors and detected a free meal.

"There are too many of them down here," Callisto said. "We need to move."

"Let me try something."

McAlister pushed the throttle forwards. The shuttle surged. The slug recoiled, one armored tentacle reaching out.

Callisto cried with rage as the shuttle's left wing was enveloped in a blaze of plasma. McAlister was already fighting with the controls, trying to compensate.

"Can you navigate us out of here?" she asked. "If you can get us into orbit, I might be able to find us a ship that can outrun those things."

"No promises, but I'll try."

More slugs appeared. They hunted by sensing disturbances in the fabric of space-time produced by large masses—and the shuttle was proof enough.

"Take us up!" Callisto yelled. "Hard! Harder!"

"Easy," McAlister said, wrestling with the controls. "We don't want to get into a stall."

The shuttle's drive faltered, then came back on again; they were thrown against their straps. As the shuttle tipped and bucked, McCalister jabbed the control stick into its flank. "Hang on."

The shuttle bucked again.

"You all right back there?" Callisto said.

"Yes," Scorpio said.

Suddenly a slug lashed out with its forelimbs, scrabbling claws catching hold of the shuttle's landing gear. The slug's body was armored in self-healing chitinous plates, and McAlister knew that even a glancing blow from his shuttle's fusion exhaust would probably cauterize wounds without doing any actual harm. He watched the slug's head track the maneuver, trying to judge where to bite.

"Where the hell did it come from?"

The slugs were designed for planetary engineering and terraforming projects and were very good at what they did. The only reason they were ousted from Earth was their propensity to kill humans. Their temperaments were poor; they were paranoid and murderous. They would not hesitate to kill an intruder if cornered, but otherwise, they were as timid as rabbits. The ones on Mars were older than most, their hides scarred by micrometeorites.

McCalister tugged the stick back, pulling the shuttle into a steep climb. He was familiar with slugs from his time in the service. Subtle differences distinguished half a dozen varieties. This one was probably older. He hoped it was not capable of breaching the shuttle's hull.

"Shit," McAlister said, veering away from the creature's strike.

Callisto cursed, too. "This is going to get crazy."

"No slugs around Phobos?"

"They never made it there, or we'd have seen them by now."

"You've been to Phobos?"

"Not me. My parents, yes. But that was long ago."

McAlister nodded. There was a sudden lurch. A report, like distant gunfire. Then nothing.

Callisto glanced at McAlister. "We're going to die, aren't we?"

"We're not going to die," McAlister said, hoping it was true.

The Aurora settled back down. The shuttle's systems gave a subdued burble of relief as it reassumed its default configuration.

A green diamond of light appeared.

One of the hull armor tiles had been ruptured by a scimitar tooth. The hole was triangular, but the edges were ragged, glowing with hellish incandescence. The canopy blushed a bilious green.

Callisto seemed to expand in her seat as if something was pumping up her restraints. McAlister felt they were about to hit something hard. Then the shuttle lurched again. This time he was thrown against his restraints. The shuttle slewed round in mid-air, and then they were falling—fast—towards the rust-streaked ice of the lower atmosphere. McAlister's heart was pounding, and he was starting to think they would crash.

"We're going down," McAlister said.

Callisto's face tightened.

They reached the crest of a final wave, and then there was a wall of seething black and silver just in front of them. They hit it head-on, the impact juddering the entire shuttle, which now behaved more like a leaf than an aircraft. They slid through and were descending at an angle now.

All the light was gone.

The slugs had pierced the shuttle's belly, slashing a white-hot cavity in its hull. It was this hole that sucked in the gases from the engine, freezing them into a solid plug. And the plug was traveling with them, wedged tight into the black hole.

The shuttle fell into the planet, tearing through a layer of moss-green clouds.

The shuttle was designed to descend at several G's.

A crack of displaced air.

In another time, he would have enjoyed this.

He looked back at Callisto, her face grey, hands gripping the armrests. The shuttle shook. There was another distant, muffled explosion.

She turned to him. "What was that?"

He didn't have an answer. A slug's head flared into a hemisphere of light, a dazzling blue that must have been several hundred degrees. McAlister raised his hand against the glare.

Its back end was studded with articulated gripper arms, which could tear the shuttle to shreds.

"We need to get out of here," McAlister said. "We can't take that thing on."

They were past the point of no return. The shuttle's hull would soon be breached.

"Well, at least we're not going to hit it at speed," McAlister said. "Let's get out of here."

He felt the craft jolting back and forth against the sand. He had not expected it to land so well.

"It was fun while it lasted."

He twisted in his seat and braced his back against the wall. "Are you all right?"

"I'm fine," she said, sounding rattled. "What do we do now?"

McAlister slumped back. "I suppose we shouldn't wait for them to kill us."

The fore part of the slug had buried itself in the red sand of a dune. The tail section reared up, questing, almost as if the thing was trying to spear the shuttle. The rear half of the slug must have hit the shuttle while it was still in the air.

A white slug crested the shuttle's windscreen and reached toward the cabin.

The mouth was a dark chasm edged with teeth. It opened wider and wider, a smile splitting its head. McAlister braced himself for the worst. The slug crashed into the shuttle's passenger compartment with a sound like an axe being swung at a block of wood. The shuttle lurched, the slug thrashing at the outer hull.

It had almost reached them when its attention was drawn to the shuttle's shadow. McAlister wondered whether it was all over when he saw the slug rearing up. The slug had seen the shuttle's shadow and must have concluded that the moving black blot on the ground was more interesting than the cold patch of shade it had been investigating. McAlister felt the tug of acceleration as the shuttle lurched forward, clearing the dune's edge. It slewed sideways, sending up a massive surge of red sand.

Then it broke into the mouth of the fissure. For a moment, the slug blocked its path. Then the thing eased its bulky head around the vessel's nose, seeking out the crack where the door was hinged open. Two segmented arms uncoiled from its head. McAlister could see them flexing as they extended. He was dimly aware of his first mate Scorpio tapping commands into the console and the shuttle's machine gun locking onto the slug.

He fired.

Little pieces detached themselves from the parent body and wriggled towards the crash site.

"Is it dead?" McCalister asked.

"Almost," Scorpio said. "The white slugs are weird—and clever—they never die in the traditional sense. They just keep growing back."

The white slugs had detected the shuttle's hull emissions. They came to investigate.

They were going to be very disappointed.

Scorpio reloaded and fired again.

The hull vibrated with the firing of a second round. They watched the second slug disappear.

"I guess we can call it a tie," McAlister said. "That should be more than enough to keep Galaxica happy."

Callisto gave him a black look. "It's not a tie," she said. "It's a stalemate."

"Same difference. We still have the old blackout bomb, don't we?"

"Not anymore," Scorpio said.

McAlister said nothing.

The slug flinched. White smoke unfurled from its rear, spinning it round in mid-air. The segments struggled to stay joined. The gap in its side closed like a zipper. Then the pieces rejoined, white tendrils undulating in mid-air.

Callisto watched McAlister rise from his seat, his boots kicking up a cloud of ice crystals from the frosted hull. She hesitated for a moment.

She turned to Scorpio "Can you get Galaxica on any frequency?"

"I'm trying," Scorpio said.

McAlister checked his display. Scorpio was scanning the network, trying to figure out what Galaxica was doing. She had not responded to any of the ship's distress calls, which was worrying. He changed frequency and made contact.

"McAlister," Callisto began, "you're close now. You just have to hold on."

"What if the creature damages the ship again?"

The two remaining slugs had stopped probing the ground ahead but remained coiled in the same positions as before. They were overseeing McAlister and Callisto as though they sensed fear.

McAlister stopped the crawler a couple hundred meters short of the slug's burial ground. He and Callisto dismounted, each taking an air bottle from the crawler's emergency supplies. When the doors slid behind them, they inflated their pressure suits and secured their weapons to their belts.

There was a burst of white noise from his earpiece, and then he heard a crackle of radio transmission. "We've lost contact," Galaxica said. "No one's responding to my signals."

The ground sloped away from the rim. Perhaps five meters down, the rind of black glass looked solid, but as the three of them neared it, McAlister began to see thin fractures in the surface. There was a fracture about one and a half meters long at waist height. The edges were sharp.

"We need to go back," McCalister said.

BREAKING TABOOS

The time came when McAlister could take no more of the world. He knew that he was breaking a taboo, one that could never be spoken, and so he was very careful not to say it out loud. It was the reason he could not simply slip out of the base and go home. There were Anarchos there who needed him.

And now the old dream was returning. He would always be an outcast from his people. It was a truth he would have to accept.

Later, in the Aurora, McAlister unpacked his medi-kit, swallowing the antibiotics and anti-nausea drugs he'd neglected to take in the haste of the escape. Then he unpacked the weatherproof gear, vacuum bags for their bodies, and electronic equipment. Callisto took her medications. They climbed into the first vacuum bags and sealed them.

He opened the shuttle door and felt the suit harden itself around him. The membrane did not vanish but retreated a little way. It still seemed to be holding its own against the atmosphere outside.

Callisto followed, struggling through the membrane that clung to her with tenacious adhesion. She bent double and pushed at the thing with her fists.

They had a twelve-hour journey ahead of them, with the prospect of a forced march through enemy territory. The Discordians had been enemies since they first formed a political entity on Mars.

McAlister put his helmet on. The visor hardened to opacity. "Ready?" he asked"

The suit began to climb his legs. He looked down at himself, confused. The ribs continued to fold in on themselves and harden. Within moments he had an exoskeleton, which was doing its best to grow downwards and outwards.

They picked their way over the hard-frozen, stony ground, boots crunching through the thin frost that had formed in the still of the Martian night. He put a hand on Callisto's arm.

Suddenly, Callisto slipped in a froth of bubbles, a dark goo suspended in a globe of thick, stinking solution.

It took them several minutes to break free of the membrane and another to pull it off. McAlister had to step on it repeatedly, stomping down on the ribs until they broke and the membrane collapsed into a slippery gel. The smell of it made his stomach turn. Callisto kicked the membrane into the dust.

McAlister crouched to inspect it, impressed by its malleability and tensile strength. It was, he thought, a remarkable example of convergent evolution—a technological mimicry of the ancient chameleon tongue.

"You are lucky, Arean," said Callisto, kicking her feet free of the membrane.

"No other shuttles would have brought you this far.

"Why?"

"Most are still crewed by Discordians. Scorpio is one of ours. The slugs would have sent their full signal by now, and they would be inundating the system with radio noise. It would take them a little while to sort through the possibilities."

There was no point in trying to fight the slugs or get close to them. But there was one way of delaying them. He slowed to a walk.

Strange rock formations were protruding from the regolith: like melted wax poured from a container and allowed to harden.

McAlister kicked one of them, expecting it to be brittle, but the surface had a kind of sheen to it. It did not break; instead, it bent like a sheet of soft rubber.

There were a few bootprints in the soil, none of them his.

"I'm no technician, but I think we've got a problem."

Callisto paused in her tracks.

"Yes, I think you're right. There's something about the schematics I don't like."

THE SLUGS

McAlister tried to judge how far he was from the wall, but the heat shimmer made distance difficult to gauge. The top of the structure was now much closer, just visible above the haze. It was a sight he'd witnessed countless times from orbit, but never up close, never at ground level.

He checked his watch. Twenty-five minutes until the first shuttle lifted off from the Mother Nest. They were an hour late.

He began to climb the tower. The surface was spongy under his boots but firm. The material that composed the structure was much stronger than his leg muscles.

He was close enough to make out the glossy black basalt that composed it. His boot slipped on something, and he pitched forward, cracking his head against the dyke. Then he was rolling over and over in the soil. There was something sharp underneath him, digging into his side.

The air was full of dust. He reached out with his free hand and felt something there hard as steel.

It loomed over him, impassive and unforgiving. It might have been carved from a single boulder. He might have been crossing a river of mercury. He kept running.

There was a crash of boot heels against metal.

He knew he'd arrived. The hull was a shallow bowl about ten meters across, its interior raw and cratered. It had been ejected from the rock with violence. There was no sign of the passengers.

He closed his eyes. The scuffed soil crunched under his feet. He tried to think like a giant, but all he could manage was an attenuated child, pathetically attempting to move a mountain.

When he'd gone still enough to think, he heard the voices.

The wind came in sudden icy gusts, twisting his footsteps and making the lights of the base of the wall ripple like the Northern Lights. McAlister felt that he could not run fast enough.

Then something moved against his faceplate. It was a slug.

He stumbled, falling to his knees. Callisto tumbled past him, making an odd grunting sound as she crashed into the slug. He looked up just in time to see a handful of movement like that of an eel.

"Close," Callisto said.

McAlister put a hand on her arm. "Get up that ladder."

He was almost at the base of it when the slug attacked.

It surged out of the sand. Callisto screamed. McAlister felt himself falling. The ladder collapsed beneath him.

He hit the ground and rolled. Sand erupted in a storm around him. The slug smashed against the tower's base and coiled around it, obscuring the view of the opening. McAlister was already scrambling to his feet when he felt the tremor of the slug's emergence through the sand. The slug was now directly above him. McAlister jumped, using his momentum to drive his boot into the slug's side. The slug recoiled from the impact, flinging McAlister away. McAlister fell to the sand. The slug reared up again, preparing to strike. McAlister's only chance was to get out from under the slug, so he jumped and charged at it.

The slug swung down its head. McAlister slammed his boot into the underside of the jaw, near where he'd seen the beast's throat. The slug's head jerked sideways, its jaw dislocated. McAlister kicked it repeatedly until the slug was on its back, thrashing, the dislocated jaw flopping against the sand like a landed fish.

The slug coiled and snapped, trying to throw McAlister off, but he stayed with it, kicking it again and again. Then he felt something moving against his back. He spun around and saw the second slug rearing up behind him. McAlister took a step away, bringing his foot down hard on the beast's snout. The slug twisted, throwing McAlister from side to side. Then he was airborne, flipping end over end, hitting the sand hard, rolling. He came to a stop, a sharp pain in his arm. He looked back to see the slug thrashing the sand where he'd been standing.

"Are you okay?" Callisto asked.

"No," McAlister said. "I think my arm's broken."

"You're bleeding."

"So are you."

He was about to say more when he saw that the slug was coming.

McAlister and Callisto stood side-by-side and aimed their weapons.

McAlister squeezed the trigger.

The wave of blue fire washed over the slug. For a moment, nothing happened. The slug coiled, seemingly unharmed.

Then its segments began to dissolve. White tentacles writhed from the ragged wound in its side and then whipped back into the slug's corpse.

In the blue light, the slug seemed to melt into itself. It took only a few seconds. When it was done, the stench was like burning plastic.

"Where the hell did that come from?" Callisto said.

McAlister shrugged.

The two of them stood and looked at the dead slug. McAlister's gun hung loosely in his hands. Callisto's weapon was pointed at the ground.

"Do you think it's dead?" Callisto asked.

"Let's find out."

They approached it.

Its sides heaved. Then it coughed up a wad of flesh.

McAlister took a step back. He knew that if the slug had been dead before, its motions would be erratic at best. The slug was still alive and trying to digest the meal it'd just eaten.

"We should leave it," McAlister said.

"It'll be dead soon," Callisto said.

"We should go."

"Where?"

"Anywhere. We'll come back."

McAlister turned and started back toward the ladder. He looked back once and saw that Callisto was not following.

"What is it?"

"I just don't want to leave it here."

McAlister turned back. "I'm sorry, but I don't think we have time to bury it. It's just a dead slug."

"I know, but—"

"Come on," McAlister said. "It's not like it'll ever be able to hurt anyone again."

He resumed walking. She followed, the two continuing side-by-side toward the ladder's base, neither speaking.

Another slug's diamond head was oriented toward McAlister. The entrance was about twenty meters away. McAlister began to sprint. He heard Callisto and Scorpio shouting something behind him, but he did not dare look back. He stretched his stride, letting the sand fly from his feet. Suddenly, the slug was moving far faster than he'd ever seen one move. The head turned in his direction, the iridescent shimmer of chitin pulsing in the air like heat haze.

McAlister's legs began to ache. His breath came in ragged gasps. He knew he would not make it. There was no way he could outrun a slug. The thing would strike him down at any moment.

He felt something warm and wet at his feet. The slug had extruded a single white tendril from its diamond-shaped head. The tendril stretched toward him. McAlister looked down at his feet and saw that he'd stepped in a patch of the slug's slime. He was covered in it. He was too close to the slug now to get away. There was nowhere left to run.

And then the slug's head exploded, the sound echoing down the canyon.

The force of the explosion knocked McAlister to the ground. He crawled backward, trying to get away from the main body of the slug. The creature's body coiled around him. It was still moving but sluggishly. White tendrils writhed like disembodied tentacles. McAlister struggled to his feet. A plume of steam rose from the carcass. It hissed and sputtered.

He looked around. A colossal figure stood silhouetted in the mouth of the entrance. It was like a statue made from a melted candle. A slug-segmented body was coiled around its left leg. A laser scalpel glittered in its hand.

McAlister stood in silence. The figure walked toward him, stepping gingerly over the dead slug. McAlister knew that the figure must be one of the hooded, yellow-eyed natives of Mars.

"You're . . . one of them," McAlister said.

The figure stopped, raised its free hand, and pointed at McAlister's face.

Its movement was like that of an eel.

Then it was gone. Another slug snapped its jaws, but McAlister was already past it. He turned and leaped onto the slug's back. In his right hand he held a neural lance.

The slug's hide was highly sensitized to the electrical fields human bodies generated. McAlister had a moment to marvel at the slug's muscular heft—it was a meter and a half thick here, tapering to half a meter at the front—and then he stabbed his neural lace into the slug's brain.

The creature went rigid. McAlister rode it like a cowboy, his boots digging into its hide. He took hold of the diamond-shaped head and twisted it as far around as possible. Then he jammed the head into the sand, pinning the slug to the ground.

"I have it," McAlister said.

But he spoke too soon. The slug pulled its head out of the sand and coiled back. Callisto stood in the shadow of the slug's coils, looking up at the ragged diamond-shaped head.

Then the slug's segments began to dissolve. White tentacles writhed from the ragged wound in its side and then whipped back into its body. Gas began to boil and freeze in the spaces between the slug's coils.

He saw Callisto lying motionless in the mud, a halo of dark fluid spreading from beneath her. Then another slug emerged, and Callisto's body became a side-glimpse seen from a different angle, like a painting or a three-dimensional model viewed from a new perspective.

The slug pulled back, presenting McAlister with the illusion of flight. It reared up again, taking her head with it. It then swallowed the rest of the body whole.

Now there was only mud, darkening and expanding, a thousand years of frozen *terroir* cracking like ice and pouring through a sudden and gaping wound. The slug began to burrow. McAlister saw its rear end contracting as it dragged its softening body into the ground.

Then he looked up.

A crack opened in the ceiling of the permafrost, running for a hundred meters or more. The fissure was not perfectly straight but instead made a series of progressively larger S-bends, like the river in a valley, with a pair of ice-block cliffs marking the spot where the current turned at each bend. The fissure was two or three meters wide at the widest point and between two and five meters deep.

Where the crack emerged, the ice was turned to steam by underground thermals and was being vented in short, blasting jets. The water beyond the crack was white and turbulent, laced with falling blocks of ice the size of boulders. They shattered on impact, and the slabs became white water that broke against the invisible walls of the fissure.

The crack was not static. McAlister saw the slugs moving, tunneling from one end to the other, widening and deepening it as they progressed. He saw slugs crawling along the fissure walls, constantly extending the crack by as much as a meter at a time.

They were stripping the iceberg down to its bedrock. But how deep was the bedrock? It could not be more than a few meters beneath the ice, but there was no way to tell. And then the fissure opened into a cave.

Like Beowulf reaching for his sword, McAlister found his rifle, shouldered it, and brought it to bear.

The gun thumped, and a high-pitched scream rent the air. The sound was beyond pain; McAlister had never heard anything like it. It was as if some small animal was being chopped into a million pieces at the edge of an anvil. He dropped the rifle and clutched at his ears, replaying in his mind Callisto being devoured.

McAlister knew the slug had copied its behavior from some creature crawling on the ancient seabed millions of years ago. A prehistoric nightmare, something like a leech or a tapeworm, if such a thing ever existed. Something like an elephant's proboscis.

It was all over now. He looked around at the scorched grass, the crushed bodies, the empty air where the slugs had been. The emptiness made him feel sick, and his knees gave way. He sat down hard, sliding down the sand. His skull ached, and there was a sharp pain in his shoulder.

The silence was terrible. He could still hear nothing but the rush of blood in his ears. He was still alone on the dried-out seabed, abandoned.

Then he heard a single, far-off sound. He did not know what it was, but it seemed familiar. It took him a few seconds to realize what it was: the movement of another slug along the shore of a runoff pond approximate to the wall.

SURVIVAL ON AN ALIEN SHORE

When the slug reached the shore it submerged. Its shadow slipped under the water. McAlister watched as the ripples slowly faded, then realized that the water had begun to boil. Something was happening beneath the surface, something more cataclysmic than the movement of a slug.

There was a vibration in the ground that felt like the first moments of an earthquake. He heard a loud bang, a gunshot-like noise.

A geyser of mud erupted from the lake thirty meters into the air. For a moment it hung there, then a shock wave knocked McAlister off his feet and rolled him away. The air was filled with a haze of silt and steam. His eardrums were ringing. He saw a figure come walking through the haze, a figure that looked very like Ersa Callisto.

"It's me," Scorpio said.

McAlister's skin tingled, and his vision sharpened. It was no longer night. A sharp electric light was everywhere, brighter than anything McAlister had ever seen. He looked up. The sky was a deep red, pulsing with black motes. They swarmed above him, an endless river of insects. Other figures appeared: Anarchos. Then he saw something he would never forget: a point of white light in the reddish sky. The brightest point of light in the entire universe.

The Anarchos opened fire. McAlister grabbed the edge of the wall and began to haul himself up. It was difficult; the angle was awkward, and he could feel the rim of a slug's mouth closing inexorably against his boots. The gunfire stopped. The slugs around the nest fell still. He pulled himself up, dropped to his feet, then stood gasping.

There stood Galaxica. She reached up and opened the visor of her mask. "You must leave now," she said. "They won't attack you if you don't attack them."

McAlister looked around.

"There must be thousands of them," Scorpio said.

"I know," Galaxica said. "If you start fighting them, they'll attack and kill every last one of us."

McAlister could see the fear in her eyes. She was right to be afraid. The slugs were terrifying: utterly inhuman and very large.

"Okay," he said. "We'll go."

The slug's slime darkened the sand around his feet; he brushed himself off as best he could.

"You can walk?" Galaxica asked.

"I think so." He held out his arms and turned in a circle, testing his joints. He could still feel the tension in his arms from the forced exertion of the flight, but otherwise, he was okay.

"We'll head north," Galaxica said. "The slugs will let us pass, as long as we don't provoke them."

McAlister nodded and looked around. He could see the other Anarchos, huddled at the lip of the nest, waiting to be told what to do next.

"Are you all right?" he asked.

Galaxica nodded. "I think so."

"You have my sympathies."

"We're more resilient than we look."

He nodded.

The slugs had the high ground.

Galaxica said, "Stand back."

Something like a bright camera flash burned at the base of the nest. The nest appeared to quiver, and the slugs stopped thrashing for a moment. Galaxica raised her arm.

"Down!" she shouted.

The slugs were moving again, flowing up and over the lip of the nest.

Galaxica was counting them. "There're only about thirty. We can do this."

"They'll be on us in seconds," Scorpio said.

McAlister glanced down at three slugs squirming closer to the nest, their maws gaping, spraying plumes of sand.

Galaxica must have been looking in his direction because she suddenly shouted, "Take cover!" and McAlister ducked behind the lip of the nest.

The slugs' attention was fixed entirely on the nest; none of them looked his way. Galaxica fired her laser, and something in the nest glowed white-hot. Then there was a booming explosion from within the nest, and the slugs began to burn. The blast pushed them back, blackening the sand around the nest's edge. Something dark and hard flew out of the nest and arced up into the sky. A few moments later, it began to fall, trailing smoke.

Galaxica yelled something, but the explosion had deafened McAlister. When he looked up again, the nest was ablaze. The slugs had retreated, and the three closest to the nest had turned white and wisped away like morning fog. Then something massive rose out of the nest. McAlister glanced at the other slugs; they had halted, perhaps a hundred meters from the entrance.

The front of the nest was still ablaze, but the rear was intact. The something that rose from the nest was climbing out of the back, charred and blackened. It was a massive slug, and it sloughed off its burnt shell in a matter of seconds.

The slug surged forward. McAlister fell flat, pressing himself into the sand. The slug covered the distance between them in a matter of seconds; now, it was directly overhead. He looked up; saw that the underside of the slug was corrugated, like the surface of an ocean wave. Hundreds of diamond-shaped teeth ringed its maw. The creature's teeth were not for chewing: they were for ripping.

The slug dived, burying its teeth into the sand. McAlister could hear its internal machinery screaming, a loud chittering sound.

It was then that he saw the drones, two of them whirring down out of the haze. He remembered something about drones being too large to fly in the nest; they had to be ejected, like wasps from a hive. The first drone came down on the slug's back, striking sparks from its carapace. It was an instant before McAlister realized that the second drone was heading straight for him. He looked up just in time to see it slam into the slug's maw. The slug bucked and threw the drone into the air. It struck the ground some way from McAlister, its wings windmilling before it was finally still.

The slug drove on, almost at right angles to its original direction of travel. Then, with a shuddering gasp, it buried itself headfirst.

Galaxica's people kept firing at the slug until it disappeared. Then they turned their attention to the two dead machines, which were nothing but smoldering wreckage.

McAlister picked himself up.

Something like a bright camera flash burned at the base of the nest. The nest itself appeared to shift color, darkening as it dilated. McAlister had to look away, even though his visor's filters could have handled the glare. When he looked back, the nest was gone, as if it'd never been. He realized he could no longer hear the slugs. He'd failed to noticed the noise they made until they were gone.

Galaxica's people stepped away from the hole. McAlister walked towards it, testing the sand before putting his weight on it. He heard a small sigh from below, almost as if someone or something was relieved.

Galaxica turned to him. "Well?"

McAlister nodded. "How deep is it?"

"About a hundred and fifty meters. We'll have to climb down the outside."

McAlister turned to the other Anarchos. "I need rope. Lots

of it. We don't want anyone to fall."

McAlister waited until the group had gone to fetch the ropes before walking back to the base of the hole. He was not worried about the slugs.

Galaxica's people would be safe enough while they stayed on the surface, and the slugs were too busy with the nest to be able to spare any attention for anything as small as McAlister. He knelt and put his helmet against the edge of the hole.

"You coming?" Scorpio asked.

McAlister looked up. Scorpio was hovering near the edge of the nest. His shell was as black as ever, but his manipulators shone a brilliant crimson.

"What about you?" McAlister asked.

"I don't like it. Too much sand, not enough rock. But I guess I have to come. It's not as if I have a choice."

THE DEADLY DANCE

It was a strange-looking gun, black and ovoid, studded with devices and dials. He saw the man's hand flex, saw the gun shift to point directly at his head. A second passed. The man's finger whitened around the trigger. Then he slipped off the rope and toppled past him toward the slugs.

McAlister held him by the arm, his fingers dug into the joint, trying to halt the man's momentum. The man spun like a falling leaf. He could feel the man's bones moving under his fingers, even his shoulder blade and collarbone as if they were articulated parts of some bizarre machine. The man fell toward the gaping maw of a slug. There was nothing McAlister could do. He looked at the man's falling figure, watched the soles of his feet, the legs bent in the falling position, and saw the body, face down, turning, falling. There was no way to know if the man had managed to get off a shot.

McAlister almost lost his grip. He was now dangling by one hand. The ladder was swaying from side to side.

One of the other Anarchos shouted something, but the impact's vibrations shook his voice into incoherence. McAlister saw a black shape rushing up toward him. The form smashed into the ladder, wrapping around it like a metal tendril. Then it was past him, and McAlister could see that it was a rope ladder being lowered from the top of the wall.

The man at the top was lowering himself down the ladder. He shouted something. The man who had been falling was only a few meters below him. McAlister looked down, but seeing the man's face or any part of his body was difficult. The falling man was very small. Then McAlister realized he'd fallen into the slugs.

McAlister felt something sharp in his hand. He looked down and almost lost his gun. In the confusion, he didn't even noticed. He was only now realizing what happened. He was holding the dead man by the arm. It was like grasping a broken branch.

As the two of them dangled, locked together, McAlister saw that it was a gun like the one Galaxica gave him. The Anarcho raised his other hand and squeezed McAlister's shoulder.

He's alive, McAlister thought.

McAlister let go of the ladder and groped for the wall, seeking handholds.

McAlister tried to breathe normally, but his ribs hurt. "We're getting him out of here, then?"

The Anarcho shook his head. "There are at least a dozen more slugs in that nest. They'll be coming out here soon. If you want to take him, you'll have to take him now."

McAlister looked down and watched the dust kicking up around an injured slug. It was about the size of a pig, but thicker in the middle, tapering toward the two flat ends. Two large antennae protruded from the top of the slug, and the base was mottled with a sparse covering of pinkish-red fur.

A million thin filaments sprouted from the bottom, most of them just a few centimeters long but a few longer than a man. As he watched, a second antenna broke free from the slug's flesh, lashing at the group of Anarchos.

The other Anarchos opened fire, filling the slug's hide with bullet holes. The slug thrashed, dislodging rubble. McAlister watched the wounded slug lash its tail, watched a black fibril unfurl from the tip, striking a woman who had fired at it. The filament whipped the woman's arm off at the elbow.

She fell, clutching at her ruined arm.

"No!" screamed McAlister.

He dropped the gun; later, he didn't remember doing it. He fumbled in his pocket, fingers scrabbling for the ring.

The injured slug unwound itself from the pit, rising like a cobra.

It was half-eaten away along one flank, but the damage didn't seem to be affecting its ability to move. The antennae lashed out again, whipping at the fleeing Anarchos. The woman fell, struck by a spar that ripped through her torso.

McAlister glanced toward the ladder. He saw two Anarchos, blue pressure suits barely distinguishable from the rest of their black-uniformed bodies, climb over the rim of the wall and head toward them.

McAlister climbed another rung, then glanced back down. The slugs were coiling around the base of the wall, twitching their spiked hides in a slow, menacing dance.

McAlister climbed. His legs were trembling, and he could feel sweat breaking out all over his body. At the rim, he hauled himself over the edge of the wall. A pressure-suited Anarcho reached down to help him. He thought he heard a dull wet noise from behind, where the man was helping him up and out of the way. A few seconds later, a team of Anarchos pulled the injured Anarcho up and over the rim. Then they dragged him away, his pressure suit turning a wet crimson as the blood spilled on it began to freeze. McAlister had to grab hold of the wall to steady himself.

"He'll live," Galaxica said, materializing next to him. "It'll touch and go, but he'll make it."

INESCAPABLE TRUTHS

He stumbled toward the spacecraft. It was ready to fly, its hull already pressurized, its fusion engines fully charged. McAlister peered through the forward viewport; he could see Ersa Callisto's body, almost unrecognizable now that the flesh was burned away.

How was this even possible? He'd seen what happened to her.

He did not want to go back to the Mother Nest; he did not want to see Galaxica again, or talk to her. He wanted only to be alone, to think.

I don't know how to feel about what I've done. When Galaxica told me we had to escape, I went along with it. But at the same time I felt…ambivalent. Did I feel guilty at having to leave our friends behind? Yes, but not as guilty as I might have. I'm not sure why. Because it wasn't just my friends; it was every human being on the planet. All of them dead; even those who hadn't been evacuated. That means—it means—what? That there was never going to be a chance for them? That they were already dead before the slugs arrived? No. That's not it. It was a lack of...choice. None of us had a choice. We were rats in a cage. Even now, what are my choices? I could go with the Anarchos, I suppose. I could fly back to the Mother Nest, and surrender to them. But even if I did, I'm not sure I'd feel any better about myself. I'm not sure anything would make me feel better. There's a part of me that thinks...that thinks everything I did, all my life, everything I thought I stood for—it was all just a game. A game I thought I was winning, but I wasn't. I'm not sure what the game was. Not any more.

MYSTERIOUS MOTIVES

Galaxica consulted her console. "We're fine for delta-vee, but we'll need more than half our remaining reaction mass for deceleration by the time we get there. That's not a problem. The issue is that our tanks are only a quarter full. We can make it to Phobos, but we won't have any margin for maneuvering once we arrive. We can't afford to be caught out by the slugs."

Galaxica knew they were a constant threat; they had been since he'd been flying out from Earth over two centuries earlier. They were not an issue in low Earth orbit, where the planet's magnetic field held them at bay, but as soon as a ship rose above the ecliptic, it became vulnerable. They had few physical forms—just long, sinuous ribbons of a smart material that could writhe into any shape and mimic any texture. What they lacked in variety, they made up for in sheer perversity.

Each slug was a different individual, which had been imprinted with the characteristics of a specific human being at some point in its life. This was how they found targets to attack. But despite this basic cleverness, the slugs were easy to elude. They moved slowly and were easily outmaneuvered. And in the decades after the war, they had become a dwindling menace: like Earth itself, the solar system's population had fallen.

"So," Galaxica said. "We need to find a way to refuel, without risking ourselves."

The old rover looked seriously damaged; they were already several solar days late in getting back to the surface and would be further delayed if the ground crew at *Valles Marineris* could not fully operate the solar arrays.

And the idea was simple: bring the Aurora battalion down to the surface, get the men and women of the other four expeditions to the surface, and put them all together in one place. Galaxica would never be able to argue with so many witnesses to the Anarchos' non-hostile intentions. They might not even try. And then the United Nations would indeed have to agree to everything he said.

"If we could find a way to get all four of them to the surface—" He trailed off, thinking about the considerable effort that would be involved. Phobos was only intended as a diversion. It would take years to prepare a new base on Mars; even longer to build a ship to take the expeditions back to Earth.

The war had taught him never to underestimate human tenacity. If the politicians could be persuaded that it was worth the effort, the UN would surely do what was necessary. The difficulty was persuading them. And if they were convinced, there was every chance that the expedition would be a success.

The members would be together and share a common goal; there would be no more room for doubt. They would not have to endure the long years of slow, agonizing attrition that had characterized their predicament for the last decade. The chance of success would be much higher if only they could all be in the same place. But he had to make sure that the risk was worthwhile. He had to know that it was a plan Galaxica could not object to.

McAlister did not understand why the Anarchos were going to such lengths to antagonize the Federation. Galaxica had refused to explain it when he'd pressed her on the matter; something about the mathematics involved. Now it was his turn to keep his peace. As arranged, Stephen was already waiting for him at the edge of the Federation colony. McAlister had never known his older brother to be much of a talker, but even by those standards, Stephen had been unusually taciturn since their father's death. McAlister could not help but feel some responsibility for that. The two of them had never been close, but he'd at least tried to understand Stephen's obsession with their father's murder.

BROTHER TO DRAGONS

Galaxica left McAlister a small autonomous surface crawler. He could drive it out of the nest and across the plains to the Federation colony if he could keep it from getting stuck in the red sand.

It was getting light. The early morning frost was dissolving into a fog. He drove across the nest, feeling the vehicle shudder and rattle. The parts of the vehicle not yet frozen creaked and squealed in protest at every movement. He kept a running commentary for the other Anarchos, just in case the atmospheric processors failed. The crawler lurched and scraped down the ramp and across the nest's inner ice field. Its headlights barely picked out the way ahead. He kept his hand on the driving controls, ready to make any adjustments in steering that the crawler's computer might fail to make on its own.

There were a few obstacles. The colony was close now, the rising sun casting a pinkish tinge on the fog. The crawler shuddered.

McAlister nodded and looked away. Stephen stood in the dust. Simultaneously, his image appeared on the rover's monitor.

"What are your plans?" Arean asked. "I presume you'll keep an eye on me until the end."

"No, not really," Stephen said. "We know where you are, and we can guess what you're going to do. We won't try to stop you, if that's what you mean. In fact, it's something of a relief to us. We were worried about what you might do."

"So what happens now?"

"I guess we just wait. Watch. Maybe pick up the pieces afterwards."

"Do you know what my plans are?" McCalister asked.

"Something dramatic, I think. If we were the ones who'd pulled you out of hibernation, we might even call it suicidal." Stephen paused as if expecting his brother to respond. Stephen continued when he did not. "I assume you want us to leave you alone for a while. We can do that. But you should know that the Mother Nest isn't just sitting on its hands. Every set of interstellar probes we've got is being diverted to the problem."

McAlister said nothing.

"Oh, and we'll be in touch," Stephen added. "We'll be keeping an eye on your communications, Arean. Just in case you come up with something."

McAlister nodded. Perhaps it was Stephen's betrayal that McAlister most resented, more than the deaths of his wife and children and the massacre at Tharsis. But there was no time for that now. He was already alone; he would be alone until the end.

It was a struggle to return to the present, to escape the vortex of his memories. He shook his head and asked Stephen about the slugs.

Stephen said: "That was a terrible oversight. In all those years the damn things never showed themselves like that."

"Why not?" McAlister could not prevent himself from leaning closer.

"We thought they might have perished. Perhaps they did, but somehow they learned to be dormant, to wait. Only in the last few years did they feel it safe to emerge again. They must have grown in number. There were always only a few hundred, nothing more. We'd seen signs, of course. The slugs have an intelligence we're still trying to fathom. But the signs were just that—signs. Patterns of activity. Until recently we had no idea what they meant. There were structures under construction in the nest, but it wasn't until the old queen died and we saw the usual transfer of her memories to her daughters that we began to understand."

McAlister looked away for a moment. "That's why the shuttles are ready?" he said.

"Yes. But they're not going to the Phobos relay station. Galaxica's made a different decision."

"Not the Phobos station? Somewhere else? Somewhere else on Phobos?"

"No. Phobos has no atmosphere, and therefore no weather, and it has no significant magnetic field. That means it can't retain an atmosphere and can't support an ecology. No ecosystem, no life. Nothing to hide behind. Nothing to block an infestation of slugs. It's just an exposed lump of rock, and that's all it will ever be. No, Arean, you can forget about the shuttles. There's no point in them ever reaching Phobos. No point at all."

McAlister nodded to himself. He'd known this, but hearing

it from Stephen's lips was another thing entirely.

"So you don't see the shuttle mission as worthwhile?"

"No. It's too late now, and anyway you're too few to succeed."

"And the alternative?"

"Go home, Arean. You've done what you came to do. And so have we."

McAlister felt a surge of indignation and anger as he contemplated the bitter betrayal of his brother. His heart was heavy with despair as he realized he would now have to face the Federation on the battlefield—and under Stephen's lead. McAlister had been foolish to think peace could be achieved without struggle or sacrifice, and now the sky was alight with the fires of war.

THE FIRE-BORN

There was pure science and pure spirit. Between these two, the human was but an accident. To the Anarchos, humanity was but a distraction from the essential reality of the universe. They had perfected the mechanics of the individual soul. By separating it from the brain, they had achieved a greater perception of the surrounding reality. For them, the dream of the new-born had become a tangible reality. For them, reality had become their dream. And in that condition they did not want for anything. Except that they would not go into space.

And it was not just the Federation or the other non-Anarcho powers who now viewed them as a menace. Most of the Discordians who had elected to join the Federation were now turning against the Transenlightenment and the Anarchos, who had made their doctrine possible. The Federation itself, initially built around the Discordian Alliance, was in danger of fracturing into warring camps. And then, just as the situation seemed hopeless, something happened none of them could have foreseen.

A child was born on a minor moon of one of the gas giants. She was as much an accident as all the others. Anarcho doctrine forbade any intervention to alter the course of evolution, even though its practitioners were the greatest manipulators of genetic structure the human race had ever known.

But that was before the discovery of the fire-born.

To some, the fire-born were a threat. But the Anarchos saw in them a potential new reality. A new interpretation of the old principle of free will. An opportunity for change.

And then they began to talk of Transenlightenment.

"I need to show you something," Galaxica said.

The sleepers were hibernating, their brains inactive, their hearts still. McAlister knew this. It was an arrangement that would never have been permitted by the medical ethics of the twenty-first century, but the prohibition had become irrelevant. No one was going to wake them up; no one was going to try to wake them up. The nearest thing to human doctors were machines, incapable of performing surgery of their own volition. And even if they could have woken the sleepers, what would they have been waking them for? They were in pain, these people. People in the nest would have gladly killed themselves if they had been given the means rather than continue existing in a twilight state that Galaxica had once described as worse than death. McAlister, for one, had no desire to join the suicide club.

So they slept. And the machines were watching over them.

The air was thick with the shame of unwashed bodies and stale sleep.

"How many more are going to die before you get it right?" McAlister said.

"We don't expect to get it right," Galaxica said. "There isn't a perfect plan. There never was. But we can try and limit the damage. It will be bad while we learn how to fight back, but there's no other way to learn. It's like we're children, struggling to walk. We fall down a lot. But we get up again. We don't just lie there whimpering until someone strong comes along and pushes us over the brink. We learn to walk. And if we fall, we get back up and try again."

"You make it sound almost noble," McAlister said.

"That's how I choose to see it. You could choose to see it as murder."

"I could. But you won't, will you?"

"No. Nor will you."

For the first time, McAlister wondered whether the Anarchos might be right after all, whether the world might be better off without humanity. The notion was chilling, so he quickly pushed it aside. What would he do if he found out that Galaxica was wrong? Abandon his world? The idea made him laugh out loud. The notion of Galaxica was laughable too, but he did not feel like laughing. It was far too serious a business. He'd come here as a representative of the Federation in the hope of finding an answer. It would have to be found in the ice, not in his head. He had to learn to walk.

Some memories seemed too big to be housed in the skull, memories that should have overflowed the reservoir of his mind and spilled into the world. The lighthouse, the one in which the boy had been born, had been a hive of memory. And now that the boy had become a man, he could see the memories still in the lantern room, where the lamps flickered in their frosted alcoves.

"Is it the pressure?" he asked Galaxica. "Are the fire-born boiling over?"

"Yes, but not in the way you mean," Galaxica said. "We don't want to forget them, but there are too many for the reservoir to contain. So we take some of them and we make room for new ones. It's like defragmenting a hard drive, or emptying the recycling bin. The memories themselves aren't lost; they're just stored elsewhere, if you like. The only difference is that if we forget them, we forget everything."

"So why have you told me this? Why are you showing me these things?"

"Because I need you to understand what you're dealing with. I need you to understand that we're not monsters. We're doing what we have to do, just as you would under the same circumstances. The difference is that you can't even begin to imagine what those circumstances might be. But you will, and when you do, you'll be ready."

McAlister was silent for a moment. Galaxica was watching him intently.

"You really believe you can win, don't you?" she asked. "Not just win—triumph."

McAlister looked away from her.

"Yes," he said. "Yes, I do."

Galaxica smiled. "Good. In that case, I have a proposition for you."

"What's that?"

"Join us."

"Join you? I don't understand."

"We're an endangered species, Arean. We need all the friends we can get. We've looked into your military capability and we've assessed your strengths. You have no chance of withstanding us. The best thing you can do is join us."

"And if I refuse?"

"You're outnumbered, outgunned, and you have no defensible position."

"So you need me as much as I need you?"

"You have no idea how much."

"You know, don't you, that I can't possibly agree to that."

"You're just seeing the people who came here early, the originals. There are a hundred and eight more sleepers yet to wake up. And that's just one of the nests. We have a dozen nests like this one. There are thousands of us, McAlister. We're a force to be reckoned with."

"I don't doubt it," McAlister said. "I just don't see why I should care."

"We're defending you," Galaxica said. "We're defending Earth. It's not much, I know, but it's something. And we'll do more, in time. We'll grow stronger, and we'll learn. We'll arm ourselves and we'll strike back at the Enemy. We'll make them regret every moment they've spent in our solar system."

"I'm sure you will," McAlister said.

PLAYGROUND OR PRISON?

It was dark, and there was no one there to see him. It was a cramped series of low-ceilinged chambers, more like a prison than a hospital.

And the babies...the babies were everywhere. Babies on floors, babies in cribs, babies on pallets, babies in cots, babies on benches, babies in the arms of adults. Some were naked, some wore only diapers, and some were fully clothed in jumpsuits. They were all red-faced, wriggling bundles of pale flesh with black eyes. Like everyone else in the nest, they were bald, but their heads were enormous, swollen-looking, spilling half of their body weight into extra skull.

A few babies were crying. Many were sleeping. A few were sitting up, looking around with patient confusion, waiting for someone to come and play with them. On a pallet against the far wall lay the still form of a baby, motionless as a discarded doll. It was a girl, apparently asleep. But it was hard to be sure. She was struggling to breathe. For a moment, McAlister thought his heart had stopped.

He stared at the child, the small face, the broken capillaries in the translucent skin. It was as if he was looking at himself, as if this boy was his son. Or his grandson. The baby's chest rose and fell, rose and fell. His fingers were almost touching the boy's shoulder.

"This one is healthy," said Galaxica. "I expect she'll grow up to be an astrobiologist."

"An astrobiologist?"

"We believe in an extreme version of human expansion. We think the galaxy should be colonized, not just by humans, but by all sentient species. Everywhere we find water, we seed it with Earth life, as a kind of insurance policy against the eventual extinction of our species. Everywhere we find intelligence, we encourage it to join the commonwealth. The universe is a big place, and it's only going to get bigger. It makes sense to take our time. There's no need to rush into anything."

"But why not?" McAlister said. "Why not just colonize the solar system? That would be enough for anybody, surely. We have enough resources here to last more than a millennium. And if you really want to leave a mark, there are always the inner planets."

The chamber was as much a playground as a clinic, with toys strewn all over the floor and hordes of small children running riot. They seemed well looked after, and as he watched the rambunctious tykes chasing one another in circles for the first time, McAlister wondered if Galaxica's sense of scale might not have been a little off. He did the math, assuming two children per woman— which seemed conservative—and came up with a population figure of nearly a thousand. Then there were the children who were not running around outside and the nursery attendants who did not look much older than ten. There was no obvious place for them, no extra beds or rooms.

The fact that he could see this much meant Galaxica was probably well disposed toward him. He wondered if she'd moved the children out of the way or if he saw them only because they knew he was coming. No: there was a subtle difference in the way the children looked at him. It was not as if they were concealing themselves, precisely, but he got the impression they had been told to stay out of sight. Only the oldest children, the ones looking right at him, had any awareness of his presence.

"Where are the parents?" he asked.

Galaxica smiled enigmatically. "A lot of them are in the factory," she said. "The rest are here. Would you like to meet them?"

She raised her voice, and immediately a hush fell over the nursery. Within seconds, all the children had vanished. He saw them scamper out through a side door. Then the door shut, and he was alone with Galaxica, standing in a suddenly vast and empty room.

"You know what we want, McAlister. We've been very clear about that. But you could refuse. You could just walk away. None of us would stop you. You don't even have to come back to Mars if you don't want to. There's nothing here to stop you."

"What would happen to you?"

"Nothing." She seemed to find this funny. "We're happy with things as they are. We're self-sufficient. We have everything we need, roughly. If you went away, we'd still have plenty to keep us busy."

THE GARDEN OF DREAMS

It was like a brightly lit summer garden. The walls were hung with huge flowers. Each blossom was a cluster of bubble domes—biospheres—and each dome housed a newborn infant. Tissue-thin umbilicals snaked away from the blossoms to spidery machines that loomed in the shadows. It was like a very advanced conservatory. The flowers hung in rows, alternating with the light and the dark. One of the infants in a bubble burst. A spray of fluid—milk, blood, or water—spilled to the ground. A machine lumbered up, trailing its umbilical. It cleaned up the mess. Galaxica walked by, without breaking stride.

"Where do you think they go when they die?" Arean asked.

Galaxica didn't answer. Instead, she brought him to a large chamber filled with small dark machines. Each of the machines was holding a bundle. It was the size of a human head—and featureless. Arean looked closer and saw that the surface of the bundle was covered with sensors. Some of the machines were simple snatchers, but others—he saw as Galaxica touched one—had manipulators, and still, others had cutting tools.

"You don't like to talk about it," Arean said. "But I'm not going to pretend I'm not curious. So I ask you again. Where do you think they go when they die?"

Galaxica turned to him, a faint frown on her face. "We don't think they go anywhere. We don't know." She looked away. "If you really want to know, you can see for yourself."

Arean's curiosity was roused. "What do you mean?"

"Follow me," Galaxica said. "And whatever you do, don't touch anything."

He followed her deeper into the nest. She stopped by one of the flower-filled chambers.

"We have cloning technology. Why should we care where they go when they die?" She turned to one of the flower chambers and gestured. "This one is fresh. You can see the outline of the infant. Watch."

Galaxica opened the door and led Arean into the chamber. It was a sphere of bubble domes, and each dome held a small bundle. Some of the piles were wriggling; some were still.

All of the babies appeared to be asleep, but for one small detail: each wore a tiny replica of the adult version of the silver torc around their neck. Just a little circlet, but unmistakable. Most of the children wore no clothes at all. They were in a half-sleep, half-wake state.

Galaxica watched them with what looked like a proprietary air, occasionally speaking to one of them in low tones. For a moment, McAlister thought she might be one of the few adults with children in the nest.

"Okay, I've seen enough," McAlister said. "What are these kids?"

"We aspired to genetic unity. These are our children."

"How many are they?" he asked.

"Perhaps two hundred, perhaps two thousand. There's no way to be sure."

"What do you do here?"

"These are the best of us. These are the ones we don't put to work in the factories." She said it casually as if the nursery was a finishing school or an academy for budding diplomats.

"What do you do with the others?"

"Mostly they're given to the stars."

"Given?" He wasn't sure he'd heard her correctly. "You mean they're dead?"

She gave him a curious look. "Not necessarily. You can live in a state of suspended animation for a very long time. They're kept in cold storage on their way to new colonies. But if the ship they're on is lost—"

He followed Galaxica to the middle of the room, where three children were gathered around a much younger infant. One of the children, a boy, held the infant very close to his chest and spoke softly to it, a trickle of words, then smiled and patted the child's back.

"That's our newest one," Galaxica said. "We call him the Dreamer."

There was a long moment of silence.

"Why the Dreamer?"

Galaxica didn't seem to hear him.

"He sleeps too much," she said. "We don't know why. We've grown him from a clone of a clone, and he was healthy when he came out of the tank. His metabolism is completely normal, and yet he spends more time asleep than awake."

"And you think that's significant?"

"It's strange. He seems to be processing a lot of information while he's asleep."

"He's dreaming, you mean."

"I don't know. Maybe. I hope so."

"Why do you hope so?"

Galaxica looked at him as if he was being deliberately obtuse. "Don't you understand what that would mean? We've been trying to achieve lucid dreaming for centuries. A sleeping mind is a vulnerable mind. You can take over a sleeping mind. You can put your thoughts into their heads."

"So you want to put your thoughts into this child's head."

"Not at all. It would be much better if the child dreamed his own dreams. I just want to give him a nudge in the right direction."

"And you think you can do that by spending time with him?"

"Yes. Why not? I think it can do a lot of good. And it's worth a try, isn't it?"

"What do you think he's dreaming about?"

"We're not sure. But we think it's not random. He's communicating with someone."

The air smelled of wood polish and strawberries. It smelled faintly of flowers. He'd never known what a strawberry smelled like, but he'd always assumed it was like this.

The adult Anarchos who gathered around the children wore an air of contentment and benevolence. They touched the children's faces; picked them up or set them down; sat patiently while they tugged on their fingers, and told them stories. They carried a plethora of toys: spinning tops, building blocks, simple puzzles, soft-furred toy animals, and even one or two dolls, which seemed a bit old-fashioned in Galaxica's day. There were musical toys, too, and games, but no screen-based devices that he could see. The adult Anarchos would never allow such things in their creche.

He was the only other adult in the room. He did not know whether to be angry or flattered. He chose to be angry.

"You said this was a war," he said. "Are we still at war?"

Galaxica smiled at him, and for the first time, McAlister noticed the slight blue tint to her skin, as if the pigment was shifting to match her mood. She'd shown him this childish trick before, but he'd never taken much notice of it.

Now he wondered if the trait was some vestige of their old humanity. He'd read about ancient racial stereotypes, and it was possible that some of the Anarchos still had their old color codes. Or perhaps Galaxica just liked the look of it.

"You really don't know?"

"Come with me."

She led him to the far side of the room.

McAlister expected the wall to be an illusion, something she projected out of the ship's sensorium. It was not. The wall was hard and white and studded with sensors.

"This is the Discordian war," she said. "You know what that is, don't you?"

McAlister recognized the type of clothing worn by the adult Anarchos: baggy smocks, generous in the arm and shoulder, and usually worn untucked. A small silver badge, a pin in the shape of an acorn, was typically worn on the smock's left breast. He wondered if the children had to wear anything in particular.

"Where did the source DNA come from?" McAlister asked.

Seeing normal, healthy children out of context was profoundly unnerving. It was like seeing a picture of yourself as a boy before you knew you were the adult McAlister.

"The DNA we brought over from the old system," Galaxica said.

"I can imagine," he said.

GALAXICA'S DILEMMA

Galaxica stood at the other side of the room, next to a small girl in a red dress. Galaxica's head was level with the child's, and the girl seemed to be showing her something. The girl looked up toward McAlister. She waved and smiled. McAlister waved back, feeling foolish. Then Galaxica's gaze flicked past him, and she grimaced in irritation.

Galaxica looked around the room. "We've tried very hard to make this a happy place for the children. It's a shame that we can't make it a happier place for the rest of the crew. We are the Closed Council. We rule this nest, and it is a democracy of sorts, but the decisions that really matter are taken by unanimous consent."

"How does that work?"

"If there's less than unanimous support, it's not binding. It's as simple as that. But we've only had to exercise that power once in the last hundred years. The Anarchos who built this colony knew that a fractured crew would be a crew that couldn't last."

She drew a sideways figure eight on a tablet and began sketching in its details.

"At birth, our ancestors had a brain no bigger than this."

A cat's cradle of lines depicted the hominid brain, as complex as a spider's web. "Then something happened. This is the period of most rapid brain growth, when you have a cerebral capacity not so different from a chimp's. But we began to modify our environment during this phase of development. This marked the point when we began to receive input from beyond the womb."

Another complex diagram appeared on the tablet, two interlocking circles, one with the small brain inside the other.

"Our brains grew to fill this region. The early data began to modify the brain architecture. Our brains began to specialize, but in more complex ways than in any other animal."

She added a second figure eight to the first.

"This second growth spurt produced the human brain. It took almost four million years to get there, but once we did, we started to redesign our brains once again. Not physically, but culturally."

A tree diagram materialized at her fingertip, branching down to smaller and smaller scales.

"Every generation redesigns the human brain for itself. You've already experienced this redesign yourself, although you don't remember it."

She sketched a scene of herself sitting on a sofa together while small robots performed mysterious tasks around them.

"That was the first stage of your redesign. You didn't notice, because the changes were incremental. You learned new habits and routines, began to wear clothes and live in buildings. But that was only the beginning. Now, we're going to do the same thing for our children."

She paused, and something in her demeanor seemed to change.

"We don't need to explain this to you, because you already understand."

He stared at her, unsure if she was serious or joking. She turned and walked away as if she'd finished what she wanted to say.

"So why didn't you just grow your children in the lab?" he called after her.

She turned. "We did. It didn't work."

He hurried after her. "What happened?"

"The ones who grew up in the lab were perfectly fine physically, but they lacked the spark of true creativity. The ones who grew up outside had the creativity, but not the stability."

She took a deep breath. "The first twenty years of the children's lives were simulated within the nurturing confines of the gestation tank, where their minds were programmed by expert tuition. We thought we could engineer the genetic material that directs cell behavior during the earliest phases of brain growth, and then grow new bodies for our embryos."

He looked around at the grass, the crumbling wooden buildings, and the wires that dangled everywhere. "What happened?"

"We learned."

"You've lost me."

"If we could have made our embryos grow in the artificial

wombs, they might have developed into something approximating our own state of consciousness, but they would have been trapped in a virtual world. We'd never be able to know whether the data we'd pumped into them was the same as the data we received, or whether they were dreaming it all up. And we'd have had no way of knowing what the outside world was really like.

"This isn't what you thought it would be like, is it?"

"We thought we'd raise our young in a simplified version of the machine-generated environment we experience. In the early days that's more or less what we did." Subtly, Galaxica's tone of voice changed. "Do you know why chimpanzees are less intelligent than humans?"

He blinked at the change of tack. "I don't know—are their brains smaller?"

"Yes—but a dolphin's brain is larger, and they're scarcely more intelligent than lions, tigers, and bears." Without seeming to do anything, she made a diagram of mammal brain anatomies appear on the tablet's surface, then sketched her finger across the relevant parts. "It's not overall brain volume that counts so much as the developmental history. The difference in brain volume between a neonatal chimp and an adult is only about twenty percent. By the time the chimp receives any data from beyond the womb, there's almost no plasticity left to use."

She drew another sideways figure eight on the tablet and began sketching in its details.

"At birth, our ancestors had a brain no bigger than this." A Neanderthal child appeared on the tablet, an adult beside it. "Here's a modern human baby. By the time they're adults, the volume of gray matter has increased by a factor of ten. What we did was to build an environment that could simulate the kind of information an infant brain could expect to receive after birth."

She sketched lines into the diagram, connecting points, and areas.

"We used the neuron growth matrix to stimulate each newborn's brain according to this template."

The sideways figure eight expanded and became a fat eight lying on its side.

"Every brain receives the same post-natal data—the same inputs, in the same order. They're also provided with a data stream to simulate touch, sight, hearing, taste and smell. We had to develop a realistic model for this. At birth, the children were all effectively blind, deaf, anosmic and insensate."

He recalled what they'd learned in training about the gestation and birth of their ancestors. The neuronal growth matrix mapped the genetic template for a modern human brain, but in reverse—from the mature form back to the undifferentiated embryonic state. Working forward from the undifferentiated template made it possible to create a womb simulation. The children were born as embryos, but ones that had already received data, simulated data designed to provide the same inputs an Earth infant receives after birth.

He tried to imagine it. An artificial womb that could simulate sight, sound, smell, touch, and taste.

"We chose the first year of post-natal life because we knew that sensory data would be crucial. The information that the children received during this period is what we'd been calling 'experience.' The task was to extract an intelligence signal from this post-natal data stream." You have to conceptualize it this way. It's as if the environment is an intelligent being. It can be thought of as a kind of machine that thinks, feels, communicates. And you have to find the right inputs to enable it to output the required data."

She took a deep breath. "The first year of your life is when you are most receptive to new information, but it's also when your brain is most vulnerable. What if we could introduce new information directly into your brain, when it was most open to it?" She looked up. "In the old days we called it educating children. These days, we call it uploading."

"And the physiological part?"

"The medulla oblongata? The lower half of your brain? There's no reason to wait for an intelligent signal from the upper brain; the brain stem is as good a place as any to start."

She drew more diagrams on the tablet, which this time seemed to portray something architectural.

"You could always give them a direct neural interface," McCalister said. "Wouldn't that be more efficient?"

Galaxica nodded. "Yes, much more efficient. And we did. It was a very short step from there to uploading—we just needed to think of the body as a kind of box that holds intelligence. You could think of the uploading process as a kind of decanting. A spoonful of intelligent soup in a bowl of warm cerebrospinal fluid, and the cerebrospinal fluid becomes soup. The upload process starts at the level of this spinal cord and works up to the brain stem, the cerebellum, the midbrain, the thalamus, and so on. You only uploaded once all of those regions have been carefully decanted. At which point your intelligence is transfered from the cerebrum into the spine."

She drew her hand down the medulla, sketching out the rest of the human brain. "If done right, you become what you are now—just without a body."

She sketched a new set of diagrams, showing the topology of a generic computing architecture.

"A supercomputer of the kind we use at home has about ten to the power of twelve transistors, each of which is about one ten-thousandth of a millimeter. That's a hundred thousand billion transistors. If you spread out those transistors in a two-dimensional plane, you get an area of about ten to the power of ten millimeters, which is one hundred square meters. A human body has an area of about two square meters.

"But surely you knew this before?"

"No. No one did."

"So you're suggesting that what you have here is… unnatural?"

"I'm not suggesting anything. I'm just telling you how it is."

"I'd like to see more."

"Of course."

Galaxica led him deeper into the nest, toward the rear of the building. As they went deeper, the crowds thinned out, and the nursery became a maze of softly lit corridors and gently curving ramps. The Anarcho guides fell away, and the ramp became McAlister's own to descend. They passed through large chambers full of scientific paraphernalia—incubators, analysis equipment, sealed glass tanks containing unusual animals in liquid suspension. McAlister caught glimpses of a fish that glowed with its own internal lantern, a rat with an eye in the middle of its forehead, and a cactus that flowered once every hour. There were dismembered robots and sculptures of alien anatomy, a rearing horse with an arachnid saddle. It was all beautiful and intriguing. The inmost layer was a nest, a place of nurture and growth. But it was also a machine for turning dross to gold and finding value in the unlikeliest places.

Galaxica showed him things that made him want to believe in fairy tales. She took him to a lab where spider crabs the size of armchairs had their joints removed and swapped with prosthetic equivalents and to another where biologists bred winged slugs in glass-sided fermentation tanks.

The walls of the nest were hung with facets containing images of Galaxica and her colleagues, some from recent times, others dating back hundreds of years. There was Galaxica with other Anarcho children, all wearing spherical glass helmets; Galaxica standing with a group of elderly Anarchos, watching aghast at a nuclear explosion somewhere on the surface of Mars; Galaxica in a wheelchair in the early twenty-first century, observing the eruption of a neutron star.

A few of the older children were studying alone. Their fingers moved in complicated choreographies. Some of the younger ones were reading from flat pages of text that wafted like fall leaves on the breeze.

They moved on. The nest's internal architecture was more regular than any other structures McAlister had seen. Corridors were wide and smooth, sometimes branching into a labyrinth of rooms. Sometimes they ended in windowless doors like the one they passed through when entering the nest. More often, they were spanned by sloping bridges that McAlister guessed must be moved around by small local positioning drives. This was confirmed when he saw maintenance spiders scuttling along a network of rails suspended from the ceiling, tending to the cables and pipework.

The nest was large. He could see no evidence of the space taken up by the grown Anarchos. Although he was unsure, he suspected that the nest was a single structure, grown to a large size but not divided into separate rooms. It was a guess, but he suspected it was correct. The nest was still expanding, still being built around the initial structure.

They walked through a forest of windowless, metal-walled cylinders. Some of them were close enough to touch. Each had a hatch on the side that could be swung open. Most of the hatches were shut. They passed several Anarchos who paid them little attention. Once, McAlister heard a low moaning noise.

Other children were intent on arching floor-to-ceiling projections of snowflakes and fingerprints, delineating endless fractal branching patterns. In one corner, a girl of perhaps nine sat on a toadstool, chin cupped in her hands, watching the sun rise over a calm sea.

McAlister knew she saw a simulation; the child had a special band around her head, a wraparound screen fed from the communal visual datastore. He watched her for a moment, noting the casual, affectionate way she touched the head of the small boy squatting beside her, rapt in a handheld hologram.

A few of the older children were studying alone. Some of the younger ones practiced simple dance steps, while others sat cross-legged, heads bowed, wearing little wispy-bun hairstyles, lost in little personal worlds of their own—the room stank of many small, healthy bodies, and the sweet-sharp tang of the ubiquitous lilies.

"Do you know what she's doing?" McAlister asked, pointing to one girl in particular.

Galaxica shrugged. "We don't know yet. We think it has something to do with processing information."

"What sort of information?"

"We're still not sure."

She stepped closer to the girl, squatted down, and laid a hand on her shoulder. The girl twitched at the touch. She wore a bulky neural-interface skullcap. There were thick bundles of optical fiber and copper wire leading from it into the base of her neck and disappearing into her clothes.

"She's one of ours, McAlister," Galaxica said. "One of the first. Her name is Fiona. I'd like you to meet her."

Fiona's hands moved as if she was working an invisible loom. Her fingers were blurred as if they were submerged in deep water. The patterns she made in the air were strange, too, and lacking in symmetry.

"You think she's not human, don't you?" McAlister asked.

"She's a person, yes, but there's no way of knowing if she's still a person in the way that you or I are. I mean, there's a case for arguing that we're not people either, not in the same sense. Our thoughts are very different from those that people had just a few hundred years ago."

McAlister looked down at the girl. Her eyes were moving very quickly, scanning the room. They flicked from one wall to another, then returned to him.

"She sees us," McAlister said. "What's she doing?"

"She's not doing anything," Galaxica said. "That's just the way her brain processes information. She's an Anarcho, but she's not a true Anarcho. She was the first, but there have been others since."

"The first what?"

"The first of the fire-born."

"She's been wired up, obviously. That can't be natural."

"We had to use technology, yes. She's not a true Anarcho. She's a failed experiment."

The girl looked up at them, hands moving continuously. Her eyes flicked from McAlister to Galaxica, but she saw nothing. She'd never seen them before. The two adults were, to her, phantoms, and phantoms were not to be feared.

"And there are others like her?"

"Twenty-three. None survived."

"Twenty-three?" McAlister glanced at Galaxica. "I don't understand. Why did it go wrong? What happened to the others?"

Galaxica looked faintly uncomfortable. "We tried to save them but—" Her voice trailed away. She looked away from the girl, through the window, her expression unreadable.

"I don't know why. We thought we had them all. It wasn't supposed to be like this. The process worked with her. She's a very special girl. But we couldn't save the others. They died, or they went insane, or they're somewhere in between. We had to deactivate them. It was a mercy."

The girl was still staring at them, not moving, hands dancing.

McAlister cleared his throat. "A mercy," he echoed. "You killed them."

"No. It was a mercy."

The girl's fingers were long and slender, almost insectile, and the tips were delicate as antennae. It was a disturbing image.

"Look," McAlister said, "I understand you don't want to talk about this, but I've come a very long way."

Something was unsettling about the room and its occupant, but McAlister could not have said what. The girl seemed to have no sense of her own body, of where her arms and legs were in relation to each other and the world around her.

No tensing muscles around the mouth indicated she was smiling or grimacing. Her eyes were not squeezed shut; her head did not nod. It was as if she had no natural proprioception. Her eyes glanced left and right but never seemed to come to rest anywhere.

Then the child did the most extraordinary thing. She extended a hand toward McAlister and spoke a single word. It was an utterly ordinary word and spoken with a flawless standard accent.

"Hello," she said.

McAlister could not help himself. He laughed. It was a single bark, loud and incredulous, like a dog's. The girl looked around the room, still not looking at McAlister. She extended a hand and spoke another word.

"Hello," she said again.

"Fiona was never meant to become an Anarcho. She was born on a planet orbiting Alpha Centauri. We had her cloned. But we never told her. We never told her what we were, or what we were going to do to her."

"What is she now?"

"Fiona is—or was—a child. A very smart one, but a child nonetheless. So she's curious. Very curious. She wanted to know what it meant to be an Anarcho, so we told her. We showed her the math, we showed her the physics. She understood it all in the time it would take a normal child to tie their shoelaces. But she wasn't satisfied. She wanted to know more."

"And so you showed her more."

"She isn't a normal child, remember? So she was still hungry. We gave her more. And then more again. She just kept on wanting more."

Galaxica paused, studying the girl.

"I never intended this to happen."

CRYPTIC WHISPERS

"There's no way to be certain." She showed him the opposite wall, where a series of monitors were arranged at head height. The nearest was the size of a door, the furthest was the size of a window. Each projected an image, but they were cryptic—either pictograms or ideograms. There were about fifteen of them in total, arranged in no obvious order.

"What are these?" he asked.

"There's no way to be certain," Galaxica said. "We think they might be displays. She turns to them at random, apparently."

"But what are they for?"

"That's another thing we don't know. But we don't think they're just for looking at. I'm going to step behind her now. Don't distract her, don't get too close. Don't do anything that might break her concentration. Just watch."

McAlister nodded, and Galaxica retreated to the other side of the room. He took up a position just to one side of the girl, facing her so he could watch her hands. For another minute, nothing happened; the girl continued her slow, decipherable dance with her hands. McAlister felt a vague sense of *déjà vu*. He was waiting for something to happen, just as he'd done as a boy, waiting for the next program to load. But this time, the wait was far longer than usual. It was almost as if the girl was performing some test, seeing what would happen if she waited long enough without giving up.

Then, her hands danced again when he'd nearly lost all hope. They waved in the air just before her. It was an extraordinarily fluid, complex series of gestures. As her hands danced, glyphs began to form in front of her, wavering holographically in midair. He saw at least two hundred separate glyphs, all floating unsupported in the air. Some were incomprehensible; others were mathematical formulae. Then the hands stopped moving, and the glyphs collapsed back into swirling motes of light. They drifted away and vanished.

"I've seen the sort of neural surgery they do on the other kids. It's not like this. They use special hardware to interface with the brain, nothing like what you've got on the end of her fingers." Galaxica paused. "This isn't neural surgery. This is the other way around. We made a machine that can think and feel. Then we made a machine that can think and feel the way she does."

"She's not a machine, is she?"

"No." Galaxica looked faintly exasperated. "But she's not a person, either. There's no way to classify her. Does that make sense to you?"

"No," McAlister admitted. "But you must have classified her in some way."

Galaxica said, "I think you need to understand what this is about, first. When Fiona was a baby, we made a device that was half software, half hardware. We could have called it a neural net, but that wouldn't have told you much. The important part was that the hardware could evolve."

"Evolve?"

"Mutation and cross-fertilization, natural selection—you name it. We put the device into a simulation of a primordial environment, a world with no life at all, and we set the software running. Then we let the device work it out for itself."

Arean was beginning to see signs of intelligence in her strange movements. "I'm just guessing, but she looks like she's carrying out a very complex program of some kind."

"Why do you think that?" Galaxica sounded surprised.

"The reason is that I can see some similarities between her behavior and my own, when I'm working on a problem."

Arean looked over at Fiona. She was doing something on the floor, tapping at it with a stick. "Perhaps she's on the spectrum?" he said.

"She's an autistic savant. Her intelligence is extraordinary."

"And yet, she can't even tell the difference between herself and a plant."

"She can't."

"Then she's more machine than human."

"Not at all." Galaxica sounded irritated. "She has the full range of human emotions. She's just as unhappy as any of us."

Arean could not imagine what it would be like to be unable to tell yourself apart from an object. He looked at Fiona again, her fingers busy at the base of a nearby plant. He thought she looked frightened. "So, what is she doing?"

"It's a way of communicating with you."

Arean waited for her to elaborate, but she didn't. "She can't talk?"

"She has her own way of communicating."

Like Morse code, Arean thought for a moment. "It's a kind of telepathy, then."

Galaxica looked down at the girl, her lips moving silently. Fiona seemed to be trying to talk to someone who wasn't there. "I'm not sure. I've never seen her communicate with anyone. She doesn't respond to me."

Arean was suddenly sorry he'd brought up the subject. "What does she do all day?"

"This is it." Galaxica seemed suddenly saddened. "I've never seen her do anything else."

THE ILLUSORY CIRCLE

A few minutes later they arrived at a large circular chamber. The Anarchos were already there, eleven identical women arranged around a slightly raised dais at the chamber's center. They had the grey skin and blue-black hair of the original Anarchos.

McAlister could see at once that they were physically perfect specimens. Their thoughts seemed synchronized as if engaged in the same mental exercise. For the moment, they were all looking at Galaxica, their expressions rapt. He could feel his gaze drawn to them, too, and had to concentrate on keeping his attention focused on Galaxica. She led him toward the raised dais in the middle of the chamber.

As he climbed the steps to join the others, he felt an odd tugging in his mind. There was something in the air. It took him a moment to identify it. Then he realized he was seeing hallucinations. He stopped, puzzled, then realized he was looking at the others through the neural static of their implants. They shared his visual cortex, and what he saw was a ghostly, wavering reality overlay. The room was suddenly much more colorful, intense, and saturated. Galaxica took his hand and guided him into the center of the group. Now he was looking at a ring of smiling faces, all eager to meet him. The hallucinatory overlays had vanished.

"So," Galaxica said. "This is our honored guest. He's the one we've been waiting for."

There was no response from the others. They just kept smiling at him, eyes slightly glazed.

There was nothing for him to sit on. The lack of furniture was not, in itself, a discourtesy, but there was something about the whole arrangement that rubbed him the wrong way. He did not belong here. He was an intruder. He felt it in the air around him, in the cold gazes of his hosts. He felt it on his first visit, but something changed in the interim. Perhaps it was the presence of Scorpio, looming silently behind him. Maybe it was the lack of visible support. Or perhaps it was just the imminence of the slug burrow, waiting to consume the entire camp. McAlister could feel its presence even now: a hot, fierce pressure that permeated the very air. He felt lightheaded.

"I think you'll find this interesting," Galaxica said, breaking into his thoughts. "Watch the screen."

Galaxica brought up a schematic of the nest and began talking about logistics. The Anarchos didn't take notes; instead, they referred to a persistent data structure, a non-volatile memory map that never left the workspace of any of the individual Anarchos.

There was a hive-mind aspect to their method of working, too. Each time one of them spoke, the others listened and learned. As Galaxica's nest-sib explained some technical detail, her facial expression changed subtly: a flash of curiosity, a twitch of distaste.

GALACTIC GAMBIT

The attack wave reached the nest unscathed. It overran the closest of the artillery platforms and shattered it with directed energy weapons. Arean McAlister could see explosions blooming amid the nest's slender supports, which rippled like a field of grass in a high wind. Then the plasma moved on to the next artillery emplacement, and the next.

Arean saw fire blossom on the nest surface; inflicting damage, but not destroying the structure. It was a temporary setback only, and he was sure that Galaxica knew it. If anything, the assault would make the nest stronger, not weaker. The enemy would have no option but to abandon the artillery platforms, leaving the nest surface vulnerable to their counter-assault. It was an elegant, battle-winning move.

Except that the plasma did not move on. Instead, it veered off at an angle, hurtling toward a different part of the nest. The guns there opened up on it, erupting into blazing petals of energy. The plasma reacted like a solid object, slamming into the defensive shields and rebounding. Then it was through, scything a jagged trench across the nest surface, like a titanic blade slicing across hard cheese. The nest shuddered as stress waves pulsed across its skin.

The trench widened, engulfing entire artillery platforms. Chunks of nest structure the size of factories broke away and plunged toward the cloud deck. Then the plasma returned, lancing back and forth along the length of the trench. McAlister thought he saw things moving down there: a black, armored mass slowly advancing from trench mouth to trench mouth.

And still, the plasma came on, blazing through the nest's weakened defenses and leaving chaos and destruction in its wake. Nest weapons continued to erupt and detonate, obliterating one another.

The wall was designed to cope with the sporadic, heavily defended attacks launched against it over the last ten thousand years. Still, it had not been designed to withstand a concerted attack by a hundred or more Federation ships.

He was in free fall again, falling back to the ice. The sky had emptied of fire. The wall, already so vast, now girdled half the world. But even as he watched, the wall was moving. It had always been creeping north and south, following the slow progress of the ice. Now it was accelerating, shifting east and west in the blink of an eye. It had sensed the attack.

Galaxica was always too optimistic.

In her study of the enemy's methods, she always assumed that the wall would not only detect the attack but also know what to do about it. But that was foolish. Galaxica had not grasped the true extent of the wall's sentience nor that its actions were not under its direct control. The wall was a distributed network of autonomous machines, numbering many millions. They could work together as Galaxica had always assumed, but they could also act independently. And the fact that the wall had always moved at a stately pace before—no faster than the ice could flow—meant that the sentient machines that made up its substance could not have grasped what was happening.

It had only taken a few moments for the attack wave to arrive, but Galaxica had already run out of time.

The wall rose to meet the attack, the wave rebounding ineffectually from its adamantine surface. But the wall was not invulnerable. Galaxica's fighters, in order to shore up the wall's most vulnerable stretch, reached the zone where it was the weakest, and they were penetrating deep into its substance.

Now the wall was thickening, its sentience drawing on its resources to reinforce the defenses. In places, vast blocks of the wall had begun to move, sliding into new positions to block the gaps. It was a chaotic and unpredictable process, and the attack came at one of the wall's most exposed points. For a moment, the wall was weakening.

Then something happened that McAlister never anticipated.

Something that no one could have anticipated.

The wall was not alone.

Something else accompanied it, a second vast structure that moved slowly from west to east.

As McAlister watched, a salvo of eighty-four missiles emerged from beneath the nest, arrowing up toward the at-

mosphere to turn and chase down the rest of the attack wave
And then the wall began to glow.

The entire front of the nest became a searing white light,
brighter than the accretion disk of a tiny neutron star. For a
moment, it blazed in the darkness, outshining the stars. Then
it faded again, almost as quickly as it had appeared. A second
wave of plasma fire streaked in from the direction of the nest,
and this time it was met by a hail of missiles.

As the fireballs hit and the ablative armor of her larger ships began to smolder, the warheads detonated, blowing
ships apart in blinding flashes. Galaxica had chosen her victims
well; those who remained intact were too busy to turn their
weapons on the wall.

The sky emptied of fire. But even as he watched, the wall
was moving. It had always been creeping remorselessly toward
the equator, but now its speed had increased dramatically. No
longer a distant circumpolar constellation, it was a discrete entity moving south.

It was still moving when a Federation megaton bomb went
off. The upper twenty kilometers of the wall erupted in a single
titanic explosion, a hemisphere of flame brighter than the sun.
The shock wave compressed the air of the stratosphere to white,
killing anyone and anything that did not have a hardened vacuum suite. The ice trembled, a ripple propagating outward from
the hypocenter in all directions. The explosion sent up a col-
umn of dust so high that it punched through the jet stream and
continued to rise until it lost its coherence in the mesosphere.

As the cloud spread, it cooled, raining down snow and sleet.
Within a minute, the entire surface of the wall was raining
down soot. But there was nothing to see of the explosion

itself; only the cloud, its dimensions visible only because of the wasteland of blackened, shattered ice beneath it.

Within hours, the remnants of the cloud were gone. But the wall was still there, undamaged and inexorably advancing toward the equator.

There was nothing Galaxica's troops could do now. They had already lost contact with the Anarcho worlds, but the satellites remained in orbit, ready to continue the work. They had come too far, risked too much to leave now.

INTO THE ABYSS

Days and weeks went by. They waited for the inevitable, but the wave front did not come. The wall had slowed; it had lost its momentum. In the wake of the megaton blast, it had lurched forward for a while, but then the eruption had expended its energy and the wall all but stopped. It was still moving, but now it was creeping south at less than a kilometer a day. Galaxica ordered the evacuation of the surface ice; only essential personnel were left behind.

Now the second wave was dropping, black-armored soldiers filling the sky.

"This is our chance," Galaxica said, taking McAlister's hand. She'd been studying his face while he watched the battle; his jaw was set, his expression blank. The thought struck her that he looked like a man to whom someone had just told a piece of bad news. She let her hand drop and studied him properly. His jaw was clenched, but it was the opposite of a death mask. He thought hard, working things out.

The soldiers were forming up into squads. "Now they're just targets," she said. "Let's get moving."

McAlister nodded and let her lead him away. The soldiers were already beginning to fan out. The slugs were targeting them with abandon now; there was nothing like a coherent formation to make them lock onto a target. But the slugs were only semi-intelligent, and the Anarchos could predict their tactics with a fair degree of accuracy. It was almost as if the soldiers were being herded toward a particular point.

"We have to get back to the others," Galaxica said, glancing at McAlister.

She was starting to appreciate the depth of his distraction. He looked as if he was running several scenarios in his head, weighing probabilities. She did not like the look of that much calculation. It made his face look wizened with age.

He stopped and turned to her. "If you can figure out where they'll be safest, then we should go there. There are going to be soldiers all over this nest soon, and I don't want to be caught in the open."

"Understood."

Galaxica studied the activity of the slugs. It was obvious what was going on, but it was also apparent that they did not yet realize it. The Federation had found a way to mass-produce the slugs. The biohazard-team slugs had been a stopgap measure, but the slugs had not yet been perfected. And because the slugs were only semi-intelligent, the Anarchos could manipulate them.

"This way," Galaxica said, retaking his hand.

The slugs were drifting toward the armory.

McAlister turned to address the soldiers. "The slugs will home in on any heat sources. Get rid of your skinsuits. The armor under them is going to give off a lot of infrared."

It was a sensible precaution. The skinsuits were only good for two or three hours at a stretch. Their air scrubbers could keep them going for longer, but the scrubbers only worked when they were connected to a power supply. The slugs might have honed in on the infrared even if the skinsuits were still in place.

"Don't wait for my order," McAlister said. "They'll be on us in a few seconds."

McAlister saw some of the men hastily pulling skinsuits off their upper bodies. Others were folding the garments and stowing them away in pack-mounted pouches. McAlister reached down and drew the skinsuit off his upper body, working it down over his arms. When he looked up again, the men were moving out toward the waiting slugs.

The moment the soldiers touched down, each one began to spray the nest with bursts from their ball guns, dropping a mist of anti-slug poison. Even if it was only a mist, it would be enough to kill most slugs. Some of the canisters would malfunction, spilling their payloads harmlessly onto the ground. It was the nature of the technology, but there was no time to recycle the defective canisters.

The gun crews stopped firing and waited for the wave to engulf them. For the moment, it was a race between the slugs and the poison. Galaxica's people were winning. Most of the cannisters were bursting even as they fell. The slugs had no way of sensing the poison in the air; even if they could, their neural circuitry was too slow to allow for more than a fraction of a second's anticipation. By the time they began to react, it was already too late.

The soldiers would be leaping from their dropships for the next five minutes and dashing about the nest like beetles on a griddle, incinerating any slug within a certain threshold blast radius.

And all the while, the spy satellites would be beaming back live images of the carnage so that the gun crews could correct their aim if necessary. The nest had been designed with just such an eventuality in mind. It was supposed to be able to withstand an attack from the air.

McAlister watched the slaughter, feeling helpless. The slugs could not know what was happening, but they must have sensed something—the air was suddenly full of black cannisters, bursting all around them. A slug was suddenly only a meter away from him, and he had to think for a moment before he realized that the creature was already dead, killed by its brethren.

He swatted it aside, sending it tumbling into two others, and then he was through the wall of the nest, out into the blazing light.

"Now's our chance," Galaxica said, taking McAlister's elbow. He resisted for a moment but then allowed himself to be pulled along.

They were both carrying weapons; McAlister a disruptor; Galaxica, a compact missile launcher. McAlister's hand was shaking.

They reached the top of the nest and stepped over the lower lip. The nest's interior was a chaotic mess of tunnels, chambers, and archways carved from the same white stone as the rest of the nest.

They were barely wide enough for a human, and some of them—particularly the low-ceilinged ones—would be impassable for a grown man. Galaxica's map, rendered inside her visor, showed the way to safety.

She nodded, and he set off, squeezing through a gap that was barely the width of his shoulders. Behind him, Galaxica followed. For a moment, McAlister was enveloped in darkness.

When he reached the other side, he saw that he was in a rough circle—the tunnel opened out into a wider space, from which branched a half-dozen exits. Galaxica was waiting for him at the center of the ring.

They continued through another series of tunnels and chambers, weaving a path through the nest that would be confusing even to Galaxica's enhanced senses.

Then the nest opened out into a cavernous space, larger than any McAlister had seen. It was spherical, with a diameter of nearly a hundred meters.

There were many openings on the surface of the sphere, most no larger than windows.

He was already finding it hard to think in geological terms.

He thought of asteroids and comets as discrete objects, even if their surfaces were rubble piles of boulders and gravel.

"How deep are we?" he asked.

Galaxica said nothing. She led the way across the cavern, following one of the larger tunnels.

The sphere was thick with slugs and black blood.

With those kills, they could continue their assault.

Galaxica's words, delivered in the direction of a soldier

crouched before her, were for the entire nest. It was impossible to tell how many slugs there were in the nest or how many had been killed by the artillery bombardment.

McAlister followed Galaxica, his eyes scanning the walls of the spherical cavern as they walked. As they made their way deeper into the nest.

EDGE OF OBLIVION

He had the weapons. He had fearlessness. He had the conviction. He was the man he always wanted to be.

And he was here at the very end of the world.

Galaxica's soldiers were taking a pounding. They were trying to retreat from the ridge, down into the nest. But the attackers were still trying to get past the trench, into the nest itself. There were bodies on the ground and pieces of bodies. And there was a noise like sandpaper.

Then the firefight reached the hole that McAlister had blasted in the dome. A huddle of soldiers was trying to push back through the gap, failing. The attackers were forcing them into a narrowing funnel of fire, into the range of a cannon that was picking them off from close range. And the cannon itself was invisible now and had probably been for some time. There was a visible sign of its activity: it was chewing through the trench at a prodigious rate, blasting hunks of dirt, ice, and mangled metal into the sky. It was using the same thermal loader that McAlister had glimpsed at the crash site. There was another cannon visible now, further down the nest. McAlister picked it out of his visual field. He must have glimpsed it earlier but had not realized what it was.

It was the other end of the nest and the gun. He thought he could see the flash as the weapon discharged, again and again.

He moved down the side of the dome, trying to get a view of the nest. There was another huddle of soldiers near the end of the dome, close to the invisible cannon. But they had not fully repaired the trench. There was another blast, another explosion of ice and snow, and another scatter of corpses.

Galaxica had left the dome. She returned to the ice ramp, where the shuttle was waiting. It had a stealth system. If it kept its emissions down, it could escape detection. She'd been able to prepare the warhead, the giant laser. She'd calculated the angles of the nest and set the charges to go off simultaneously.

McAlister pulled himself forward on the slick rime of his tether and scanned for a clear line of sight. The nearest enemy soldier was maybe five meters away, the closest McAlister had yet seen. The soldier wore armor like a regular soldier's. Still, it was of a much more advanced design—it had to be—and there was something else about it, something about the soldier's stance that made McAlister's heart suddenly hammer in his chest.

He reached for his assault rifle and started firing, aiming for where he judged the enemy soldier's heart. He set the gun on full automatic. It was more a gesture of defiance than anything else. If he killed the enemy soldier, he would not accomplish anything other than hastening his death. Through the rifle's sight, he could see the bolts of his fire hitting the enemy's armor and ricocheting away.

Then the enemy soldier raised his weapon, and McAlister watched in his sight as the armor around the enemy soldier's heart melted and blackened, the edges of the hole pulsing out like some strange gray-black flower. The enemy soldier went down and did not rise again.

Galaxica would have to fight hard to take down the entire nest before the Federation could overwhelm her forces. That was why they were still here. It was not to preserve a mere promise of hope. It was to protect something far more critical: Galaxica's reputation. The nest could never be allowed to fall into Federation hands. It would be an act of cataclysmic cultural vandalism, erasing an entire society.

McAlister heard a sudden snap behind him, like a thick branch breaking, and he spun around to see Galaxica pick up a fallen soldier by the scruff of his armor and toss him into the air, away from the combat. She used him as a human shield, pushing forward to get herself behind a big ceramic egg that was pitted and stained from heavy use. Her soldiers were now firing back in her direction, trying to pick off the Federation soldiers huddled behind Galaxica.

A burst of gunfire punched through the soldier's chest, punching her forward and forcing her to use the lifeless body as a bulwark. McAlister watched as the woman's chameleon-augmented armor went to work, patterning itself to the visual profile of the man's corpse. Galaxica stood up again, holding her position. The dead soldier looked almost completely real now.

Ahead of him, he heard shouts. The gunfire had died down; he guessed Galaxica's reinforcements were almost in position. McAlister increased his pace. His left hand reached around to the small of his back and felt for the reassuring handle of his tranquilizer gun. The front of the nest was only a few more steps away now.

Something hit him hard in the back and knocked him forward.

There was a sound like gunfire.

A black spray pattern appeared on the wall to his right. Something stepped out of the darkness, moving towards him with long strides.

McAlister aimed with his sidearm and fired, but the figure was moving too quickly. The bolt of energy blasted a divot out of the wall, then fizzled against a suit of camouflage armor.

McAlister set off again, pushing through the rubble and the hanging dust. The explosions were beginning to die down. Something was making its way through the chaos, a thing like a giant slug.

"Keep going," a voice said in his earpiece. "There's a whole rabbit's warren down here. Keep moving."

The voice belonged to Scorpio.

"Right," McAlister said. "Good plan."

He pulled a grenade from his belt and lobbed it ahead, turning to run in the opposite direction. The grenade exploded, engulfing a soldier in a blinding white flash. McAlister continued running, trying to cover as much distance as possible.

Something long and silver flashed in front of him. He glimpsed Scorpio's suit of camouflage armor, slicing downwards at the thing's neck. The blow connected, and the slug recoiled, a spout of purple blood gushing from its head. McAlister kept running.

He'd barely taken three steps when something lashed out of the darkness, coiling around his head. He felt a cold prickle against his cheek, then something wet.

The thing, whatever it was, retracted, leaving behind a long thread of gore. McAlister swiped at the blood with his fingertips. It came away, smearing against his skin. It was raining down in long sticky threads.

He stumbled onwards.

McAlister climbed the ramp. There was no one left to kill. He strode into the cavern. At its far end, he saw a second cavern. From this far out, it looked no different from the nest of tunnels he'd just left, just as menacing and uninviting. McAlister stepped into the opening, and the cavern swallowed him.

He was not prepared for what he found. The cavern was a natural formation, hollowed out and then artificially lit, but it was not a tunnel. It was a tremendous domed chamber.

RISING FROM THE WRECKAGE

Ruins, everywhere. Walls that had once been pristine and gleaming, were smashed and burnt. Doors torn open, holes in the ceiling, light pouring in. Machinery smashed, bent, melted. Glass broken. Sprawled bodies. Here and there the flesh had been flensed away, and a metallic husk had been exposed. It was very quiet. As quiet as the space between the stars.

Galaxica pointed out a roughly circular hatch, like the first hatch he'd seen, only larger. It was open, and the space beyond was as black as space itself. He looked back at her. Her eyes shone like a cat's.

She led him around the chamber's perimeter to a gap in the wall where he'd noticed no door before. There was a hatch here, like the one on the lift shaft, and when Galaxica reached up and touched the handle, it opened with a sigh.

"Come on."

The way out was much steeper than he'd expected, and he had to grab the ladder's rungs to haul himself through the hatch and onto a circular metal stairway bolted to the wall. It corkscrewed downward like a nautilus shell, and he wondered fleetingly if the builders had meant it as torture. Then he realized that the view would differ from the top, and perhaps the hatch had been placed here for the comfort of anyone climbing up rather than down. Galaxica was well ahead of him, and he had to hurry to catch up with her. She took his hand and held it as they walked.

He could not remember ever having held a hand in his life before, except perhaps his mother's, and he was not sure he liked it. But it was comforting to have her touch him. It reminded him of his newfound sense of calm. She led him down the rungs and around the circular shaft, taking them steadily and quickly and still holding his hand. At last, she led him to a window, and as they stepped up to it, he stared into the crater again.

The edge of the shaft cut into his belly. He looked down, past the railing, to the grayness of the bottom and wondered how far they were from the surface now. He thought they must be very close to the ground and the far-off surface.

"What am I looking for?"

"Tell me, what do you see?"

He thought for a moment, then pointed to a tiny, gray dot below them. "That."

Galaxica smiled. "There are five more similar structures within the nest. These are the smallest, the drones' hatcheries. Others are being prepared as we speak. More are being built in the older parts of the nest, close to the central core. All the hatcheries will be completed within the next few hours. By the time we're ready to strike back, the swarm will be much larger."

"More? You've already built more?"

"We will not run. Not anymore. The nests of other dominions are already moving against the Federation, coordinating their attacks. *Epsilon Eridani* will be consumed within the hour in a storm of armed starships. You can't stay out of that. It doesn't matter whether you die here or out there—you will die, along with every human being in the system."

"You're bluffing. This is some kind of ruse. The other nests don't know you've built these new chambers."

"We've shared the plans with them, just as we shared the drive systems' designs. We can't hide anything—nothing! You know that."

He shivered again, feeling more alone than ever. It was one thing to die in the service of some vague and impersonal principle—that was a matter of duty, nothing more. But it was too much to die at the hands of Galaxica and her nest mates because they thought they could use him. His throat tightened.

"Why are you telling me this?" he asked. "What are you trying to do?"

"I'm trying to save your life. That's what I'm trying to do. I'm trying to show you that you have a choice. And not just a choice—the only choice. Stay here, and die with the rest of humanity. Or come with us, to the heart of the swarm."

"And if I choose to stay?"

"Then you die," Galaxica said. "I won't beg. Not this time. I won't insult you."

"And if I choose to go?"

"You will be operated on. You will receive the Transen-lightenment."

WHISPERS OF REDEMPTION

"So I'm finally awake?" He glanced at the cat's cradle of luminescence wrapping itself around his body.

"For now."

"There are still machines inside me, aren't there?"

She paused. "The surgery was easier than I'd expected. You heal well, McAlister. Better than I do." She looked at him with a critical eye. "There are still a few areas of disfigurement, though."

He looked down at his body; even in the faint light, he could see a tracery of surgical scars, a few puckered and angry.

The right side of his face was a mass of livid red tissue. It would have been a lot worse if Galaxica had not intervened when she did.

"I look like Frankenstein's monster," he said. "And feel worse."

The neurovirus is out of your system."

"Then why do I still feel its effects?"

Galaxica smiled.

"You're just remembering," she said. "It was always in your head, but your amygdala was doing a good job of keeping it buried."

McAlister grimaced.

"What about the others?" he said. "The ones who weren't coming to Transenlightenment?"

"They're dead, McAlister. There was nothing I could do for them."

He watched the cat's cradle of lights move around his body, searching.

"What are you looking for?"

"Were you scanned at any point since your injury?"

"No. Why?"

"Then I don't think there's anything to worry about."

"Then it's over? You've won?"

"Not at all." Galaxica smiled. "We've just begun."

"What happened?"

"It was fine for us—most of us, that is—but the children couldn't handle it. They couldn't bridge the gap between what they were and what we were. The older ones just cracked. One minute they were listening to the music of the spheres. The next, they were running around in circles and shrieking. A couple of them killed themselves."

"And the rest?"

"The rest are still alive, but they're gone. They're in some kind of limbo between being and not being. There's no way of knowing if they'll ever come back."

"Where are they?"

"No one knows. But you saw the ships leave."

"And the remaining Anarchos?"

"The adults? We're here, and I think Fiona's somewhere on the outskirts. Maybe there's one or two more, but I don't know for sure?"

"You're sure that's everyone?"

"There's no one else here."

McAlister searched his surroundings again. There were fewer Anarchos in the network than he'd thought. "Where are they, Galaxica?"

"I don't know. Perhaps they were taken, or maybe they just fled into the dark when the attack began. There's no way of knowing. And it doesn't matter."

"It matters to me."

"Why? They're gone."

"I don't believe that," McAlister said.

A look of bewilderment spread over his face.

"It doesn't make any sense," he continued I can't believe that the mother nest is just empty. There has to be another explanation."

"I've already given you the explanation, McAlister."

"Then you haven't told me everything."

"I have. I've told you everything that matters. You were right about the weapons, but the nest was empty because it was evacuated."

"Then where did everyone go?"

"I told you: no one knows."

"That's not true. You know exactly where they are." McAlister stood up, searching the virtual world for some hint of an answer.

"I don't understand." Galaxica spoke to him, but he did not hear her.

He started toward the top of the nest. His visual field resolved into the layout of a hexagonal chamber walled by machines.

"My head is killing me."

"It's the cranial implant. I removed the others. I needed to know what went wrong." She paused. "The data is in the buffer. I can show it to you if you like."

He felt an involuntary twitch of interest; he'd been half-expecting the implants to have recorded his death, or at least the end of his body.

"Later," he said before he could stop himself. "Let's get out of here first."

"No, you misunderstand. There are no other places to go. There——"

He thought she was about to say more, but Galaxica did not complete the thought. Instead, she said: "Yes, well, I suppose it doesn't matter. There's nowhere that can be worse than this."

Again, she paused. "McAlister——"

He waited for her to continue, but again she fell silent.

"Galaxica?"

"McAlister—I'm sorry."

"Sorry for what?"

"For everything. For all of it." Her voice was low, almost conspiratorial. "You don't understand, do you?"

"Understand what?"

"The thing is, McAlister—" She stopped.

"Go on."

"Most will return to their homes, but some will stay with

us. There are already too few of us, McAlister. We needed to raise the birth rate, which means accelerating the maturation rate. In a way, you've done us a favor."

"How many of you are there now?"

"About a hundred and fifty. But we're planning to split again." Looking at a monitor, she pointed at a point in the network that seemed no different from any other. "We're building a new nest a hundred kilometers from here. That's where the new batch of Anarchos will stay."

"How many?"

"Maybe a thousand, maybe more."

So many questions. So many answers he could never hope to understand.

"We can talk more, McAlister. Later."

Galaxica had gone from being a stranger to someone he could not bear to be parted from, who had offered him sanctuary: Galaxica, who looked into his memories and saw his greatest shame; Galaxica, who was now looking into his mind. He could not bear it.

"Enough, Galaxica. I'm sorry, but I have to know. Why me?"

She was silent. Though devoid of visible expression, her face seemed to search his.

"What do you see?"

"McAlister. You're a good man. The best man I've ever known. You deserve better than what you had. But that's not why I brought you here."

"Then why?"

She paused again, but this time the pause went on so long that McAlister thought she'd fallen into some kind of trance.

But she had not. "I was trying to find a way to save you, McAlister. I could see what they were doing to you. They were twisting your mind."

THE MIND'S HORIZON

He wanted to ask whether this was what he'd wanted and whether he genuinely desired Transenlightenment. But it was already too late; the ray was less than a centimeter away from his node. It filled his mind with colors and patterns too complex to process. He was awash with data, drowning in a sea of neural code. Involuntarily, he gasped. Then, the data faded, the colors died, and the connection was broken. McAlister looked at Galaxica. Her node was fading too, and he realized that the entire nest was reverting to its original state.

"You wanted this," she said. "Now you have it. But remember: you may find it a very different thing from what you expected."

McAlister nodded. His breath was coming fast. "I don't understand," he said. "Why did it have to be like that?"

"I told you: you're not ready yet."

McAlister stepped back, bumping into the transparent wall of the cell. For a moment, he was dizzy; then, his breath returned to normal, and the world snapped back into focus. He felt energized, almost manic. The nest was reassembling itself around him, and the air was full of crackling static

"Galaxica," he said, but it was too late.

"There are many kinds of spaceships in the universe, McAlister, but only one kind of warship. You don't belong here."

The voice was familiar now. McAlister turned and saw Scorpio waiting for him, framed in the doorway. Scorpio's face was the only visible part of his body; the rest was lost in the static.

"You shouldn't've come back, Arean," Scorpio said. "This isn't your war anymore. You're not one of us. You never were. You never could be."

McAlister shook his head, dizzy again. "What are you saying?"

"I'm saying that you're going to die, Arean."

McAlister closed his eyes. There was nothing else he could do. When he opened them again, Scorpio was gone. Then the cell wall melted away, and McAlister stepped out into the upper reaches of the nest.

He steeled himself. It was coming. He tried to empty his mind of all thought but found that he could not. There was a storm in his mind, howling down the link that connected him to Galaxica's nest.

He fought to block it out, knowing it would only get worse when the ray touched him. The roaring in his mind redoubled in intensity, a noise like a thousand angry voices all talking at once. The beam had made contact with his face. He reached up and touched it with the back of his hand. There was a tingle, a numbness, nothing more.

"That's it?" he said. "I expected more."

"This is the Transenlightenment. It's not something you do; it's something that happens to you."

The light in the center of the image grew brighter still, washing out most of the ghostly patterns of light.

"This is what the Anarchos experience all the time?"

"Yes. We call it the 'Newlife Infusion.' The structures are in everyone here. But only in the Anarchos is it so advanced that they can access the Transenlightenment whenever they want. We need to be receptive, to allow the structures to extend their influence into our minds—when we sleep, for example, or when we're especially relaxed. You can't make it happen, any more than you can will yourself to fly. It doesn't work like that. You have to be receptive. That's the lesson of the Anarchos, for those who aren't quite there yet: relaxation, receptivity. Then, when the structures in your mind are ready, they will take over."

McAlister was silent. The image in the tank was fading, losing definition. He could hear Galaxica's voice, distant now, coming from a great distance.

"Are you still there?" she asked.

"Yes," he said. "What happens now?"

"The process will begin in earnest. I will be with you as you were with me in the battle every step of the way."

THE SENTIENT SEA

The bright light trembled and pulsed, the map rippling around it. And then the light engulfed McAlister's node, and the nest vanished from around him. He could feel the current flowing into him now as if it was electric; he could hear it, too, like the sea, but louder. And then there was darkness and silence, and he was gone.

"It is you," said a voice. It was speaking his name. He did not know if it was the voice of Galaxica or some other. He did not care. It was the voice of Transenlightenment, and it was everything to him now.

He wanted to ask whether this was what he'd wanted. But it was already too late; the ray was now only a few light-seconds from his mind. McAlister saw his hands as if they were a thousand kilometers away, reaching out to touch the network. The structures in his mind were still a long way from maturity, but they were already influencing him. He felt them constructing a million subtle adjustments to his body: microscopic reallocations of mass and energy and the subtlest realignment of his mental processes.

Meanwhile, the structures in the nest were experiencing the same changes on a vastly greater scale. It was as if they were two tuning forks, each struck by the other. McAlister's mind screamed at the assault, but it was already too late to escape.

"We have found a way to make our structures more tolerant of your mind," Galaxica said. "In effect, we have given you a larger mind, with more room for adjustment."

McAlister could feel the structures in his mind adapting, twisting to connect with the networks in Galaxica's nest. They were struggling to become one. He wanted to ask Galaxica if this was what she wanted, too, but he was afraid to speak lest he distract her.

The structures in his mind were irrevocably committed to the transformation. He felt the nest's influence flooding through him, remaking him from the inside out. His body felt heavy and sluggish; his thoughts felt thick and slow. He felt the nest's structures coursing through his veins and arteries, knitting themselves into his flesh. It hurt. The pain was sharp and exquisite, but McAlister had endured worse in his life. Now the structures in his mind were responding to the nest, and he could feel the nest responding to him. He had the nest's measure. He could see it in its entirety, laid out before him like a many-dimensional jigsaw. He was thinking of the speed of the nest now, but there was a downside. He was no longer himself. The nest's perspective was a million times broader than his own, but it was also more shallow. It lacked the richness of his experience. It lacked him.

"It hurts," McAlister said.

He steeled himself. It was coming. He tried to empty his mind of all thought but found that he could not. There was a storm in his mind howling down the link that connected him to Galaxica's nest. He fought to block it out, knowing it would only get worse when the ray touched him. The roaring in his mind redoubled in intensity, a counterpoint to the rising volume of the storm in the nest. And then the contact came. There was a shock, like a physical blow to his head. McAlister's thoughts fragmented, and he felt his consciousness submerge into a golden warm bath. And then there was only darkness.

Something even stranger was happening. His sense of self was growing back. The sea receded. He found himself on the shore again, gasping for air. It was a confusion of moments, not one continuous experience. The colors returned, as did his sense of smell. There was a thrumming in his fingertips and toes and the wind on his face. He heard Galaxica calling his name and felt her hand gripping his. Her node had been engulfed too, but unlike his, it had not yet spat out its prizes.

"I was never frightened," she said. "It's hard to explain, but I was always aware that it would be this way." She sounded breathless.

"This isn't just about understanding the Anarcho experiment, is it?"

"No." Galaxica paused as if steeling herself. "We had to bring you here so that you could do this."

He said nothing.

"The link has to be severed. There's no other way."

McAlister stared at her. "No other way?"

"You're in a position to do it. Nobody else can."

"And if I don't?"

"It's not up to you. In fact, it never was."

Galaxica paused again, perhaps wondering whether to continue. McAlister nodded encouragingly. She drew a breath.

"The thing is," she said, "the experiment never worked. The link formed, but it didn't work. We couldn't use it to share anything, not really. And there was a side effect. That was the price we paid for the link. We'd lost our identities, but we'd gained something much bigger. Something we think we can now see. We'd found a way to build a machine that could grow like an organism, to bootstrap itself into sentience. That's what it was really for. That was what the link was for."

"A self-organizing computer?"

"You could call it that. I prefer to call it a pattern-forming system. It wasn't designed, you see. It evolved. And it did so in the direction we see as most likely to result in something that looked like a human mind."

To her, it was normality. The question was: was he too? Could he ever truly fit into Galaxica's world?

"You still don't get it," Galaxica said, "do you? There are no hard choices here. What we do, we do for ourselves. Not for your kin. Not for humanity. There's nothing else out there to care about."

She squeezed his hand again.

"There are no right or wrong answers. Just the answers that seem best for us."

"And that makes it all right?"

"It makes it inevitable."

ECHOES OF THE SELF

In the days that followed, McAlister learned how Anarchos experienced the concept of death. Every hour or so he would ask Galaxica a question, testing out his growing understanding on her: how much of a person's mind was transferred into the datastore; whether a copy of the mind might still be present within the original brain; whether a person might still be subject to physical pain after their mind had been copied into the collective.

He was searching for some weakness in the process, some Achilles heel that he could exploit to his own advantage. It was all a delaying tactic, of course. He was trying to put off the inevitable. But the inevitable was still a long way off.

In the meantime he kept talking to Galaxica. There were long silences when he stared into the sky and thought about the children and their new home. There were times when Galaxica spoke to him and he felt his mind reaching out to her in some way that he could not understand, a kind of animal telepathy. It was at such times that he felt closest to her.

A loud noise filled the room, then nothing.

He had time to see Galaxica before she reached out and pulled him into the next phase of her plan. Her touch was not as tentative as he'd expected.

As he passed into the light, he was suddenly reminded of all the other times he passed into a different place—the first time, when his mother showed him a beach; or the time he passed from a failing spaceship into the embrace of Resurgam's outer atmosphere; or the first time he passed into a different time, to meet Galaxica on the beach at Remorse. And then there were all the other times, on the starship, on worlds whose names he never knew, worlds of vast deserts and cities so old they remembered when humanity had not yet been born. All the time, he knew his only friend in that strange place was himself.

WHISPERS OF THE FORGOTTEN

The mind was like a candle, McAlister thought. A candle could burn for a long time if you gave it enough oxygen. But if you took the oxygen away, eventually it would go out. All the air was going out of him now, and it was only a matter of time before his consciousness failed. Maybe not even then. The fire had burned itself out in the head of a hundred thousand-year-old cave bear he'd once examined. When they'd dug it up, the skull was still intact.

He held it in his hands. He looked into the empty eye sockets. He wondered what happened to this animal's soul. He knew what happened to the animal's body. Ice, or rather permafrost, had preserved it. There was even flesh on its bones. And yet...when the diggers reached the brain, there was nothing. Nothing but a few streaks of dark slime, like dried blood.

The same would happen to him. If there was any sense to it,

he thought, if there was any purpose to what was happening, then it was only fitting that he die in a fashion similar to the cave bear. But it didn't make any difference.

And yet, for some reason, he didn't want to die. Maybe it was a desire for self-preservation, or perhaps it was something more than that. Maybe it was even possible that some part of him was still intact. That was hope, and he grasped onto it. He knew it was only hope, but that was better than nothing.

The light was gone. There was only the soft hum of the machines and the steady breathing of the girl who stood guard.

He had the vague feeling that something was missing.

He thought of his future self. Of the entity that would exist within the Transenlightenment. He wondered whether the Anarchos would see themselves as his descendants. He wondered whether they would be proud of him. And he wondered what they would make of the last two centuries of human history. It was not the sort of thing one could ask a future self.

One could only hope to meet them and look them in the eye. Perhaps that was why they invented Transenlightenment: so that, when it was done, there would be someone left who had lived through it all. They would need a witness to know what it had been like. But perhaps, in time, there would be no one left to remember the darkness before the Transenlightenment. Maybe that was the real reason for it, after all. It was not the defeat of death; it was the defeat of history. And that was a victory no one could ever write a song about. A million years from now, the Transenlightenment would be all that was left of humanity. And even then, it would not be enough.

Galaxica leaned forward, watching him. Her face was very close to his. "Do you think that matters, Arean?" she said. "Do you think that even matters?"

"I thought so once." He turned his attention to the window, where the gray rock of Deimos was now racing past.

"We are not the same people we were then," she said. "Things change."

"Maybe," McAlister said. "But the rest of the galaxy isn't going to wait while we find out."

"No, it isn't."

Galaxica smiled.

"Welcome to the war, Arean."

www.ingramcontent.com/pod-product-compliance
Lightning Source LLC
Chambersburg PA
CBHW011502170626
46814CB00008B/3006